A Big Forever

A BEYOND THE TIDE NOVEL

N DUNE

Enjoy their love story

Copyright © 2021 N Dune.
All rights reserved.

Copyright: Natalie Simmonite, writing as N Dune, has asserted her right to be identified as the author of this work in accordance with the Copyright, Designs and Patents Act 1988.
All rights reserved. No part of this publication may be reproduced, stored in a retrieval system, copied in any form or by any means, electronic or otherwise transmitted without written permission from the author, except for the use of brief quotations in a book review. You must not circulate this book in any format.
Please remember this is a work of fiction. Any names, characters, businesses, places, events, or incidents are the products of the author's vivid imagination or used fictitiously. Any resemblance to actual persons, living or dead or actual events, is purely coincidental. Any trademark, brand names, product names, or that of companies used in this book are registered trademarks of their respective owners.
The publishers, author, and this book are in no way associated with any product or vendor mentioned. None of the companies referenced within this book has endorsed the book. My books are exclusively on Amazon; if you have downloaded this book anywhere else, you are stealing.

I dedicate this book to all of you who are fighting demons others cannot see. With each day you decide to put one foot in front of the other you are walking towards your future. You are not alone. Stand tall because you are mighty and you are strong.

Edited by: Mostert-Seed Editing

Formatted by: Irish Ink Publishing Services

Cover Design by: JS Design Cover Art

As always, ladies, thank you for making my book baby shine.

Prologue

BEN

Two years ago

As I walk along the cobbles, avoiding the old tram lines, I smile at the giant stationary sentinels lining the harbourside. I imagine the sounds of the hustle and bustle this once busy port must have had with its large cranes, now left as landmarks, groaning and grinding as they worked. Ahead I catch sight of my reason for being down here on the harbourside this sunny summer evening. He hasn't seen me yet, so I take a moment to look him over as I walk toward him. He is as stunning as I remember; tanned skin, short dark hair, and tight black jeans have me biting my lip to stifle a groan. Damn, Raz is hot.

I met him last weekend, I'd been out with a few work colleagues, and my eyes had immediately been drawn to this gorgeous man dancing with a blonde-haired girl. I couldn't take my eyes off him, and when he looked up, those coffee-brown eyes captured me, taking my breath away. A few beers had given me the courage to approach him once his female companion started dancing with another man. We'd had a fantastic evening chatting as best we could over the loud music and finally exchanging mobile numbers on our shared taxi ride home. His friend, Chloe, had made me laugh with her unsubtle methods of matchmaking, and that kiss I managed to claim from Raz before I went into my flat was still seared into my memory.

We've been texting the whole week, getting to know each other, and he finally agreed to meet me tonight for a date. I take a subtle photo of him standing outside the M Shed as he turns away, looking at his phone, and then send it to my sister, Jen, who insisted I tell her where I was going and who I was meeting. She immediately sends back a thumbs up and winky emoji, pulling a chuckle from my lips before I tuck my phone back into the pocket of my jeans. I've already told her how special Raz is and that I've never felt this pull with anyone else before. I just hope that he feels it too.

"Raz," I call his name as I get closer, not wanting to creep up and startle him. As he turns to face me, a smile lights up his face, and I'm lost, literally lost to this man already.

"Ben, there you are." He closes the gap between us, and as he gets closer, I'm made aware that he is a little taller than me. *How did I not notice that the other night?*

A BRIDGE TO FOREVER

It should feel awkward as we stand here not saying anything, only drinking each other in, but it doesn't, and I might be projecting, but there is definitely interest and possibly, what I hope is, desire shining in his eyes. He gestures to the cobbled walkway in front of us with a smirk on his lips.

"Shall we head to the Salt and Malt?" His voice captivates me, and I give myself a mental kick up the arse for being struck dumb by this man.

"Yes, the table is booked for seven. It's bound to be busy," I confirm as we round the corner, walking side by side towards the large windowed container-looking building that houses the restaurant I picked for tonight. I am well aware that, like me, Raz likes curry, but I thought that I would try this seafood restaurant when he expressed how he also loved freshly caught fish. As expected for this time of year, the place is busy, and the terrace upstairs and benches outside are full of people enjoying a drink and food in the sun. The smell of fish and chips wafts from within, pulling us forwards and through the doors.

Raz stands close enough that if I stretch out my fingers, I would likely be able to touch his hand, but I know that's not something he would welcome. From what little we have discussed in our texts, I get the impression that he struggles with public displays of affection, and he also mentioned that he is no longer in contact with his family.

Once we are shown to our table, seated, and drinks

ordered. I look at Raz as he studies the menu, and I can tell he is having difficulty choosing what to order. Fortunately, I checked the menu ahead of time.

"Do you fancy sharing some small plates?" I suggest and find myself on the receiving end of a megawatt smile. Damn, I wish I could stop my heart from racing as thoughts of how to keep that smile on his face have me conjuring a future together before we've even finished our first date. This is so unlike me; it's a little scary—he's so much younger than me.

"That would be a great idea," Raz says, putting down the menu and turning to the server who has returned with our drinks. I watch, mesmerised, as he thanks the young girl and orders a few plates for us to share. I don't think I've stopped smiling since I spotted him waiting for me. The girl seems a little dazzled by his charm but hides it well, and I have to hide my smirk with a sip of my ice-cold beer. *Don't worry, love. I totally get what you are seeing.*

Our conversation is easy, and I make it my mission to find out as much as I can about him. I already know his friend Chloe plays a big part in his life. He mentions her a lot, and I can't help but wonder if they are just friends. Would he have agreed to see me if there was something more between them? I hope not.

Raz isn't that forthcoming about what he does for a living, just saying he works with computers. I don't want to push him, so I divert the conversation onto lighter topics, telling him about my family, in particular, my nephew Jason and in turn, he talks more about his friendship with Chloe. When the food arrives, we order more drinks, and a sense of comfort flows through me as we tuck into dishes of scallops, sardines, and sourdough. The little noises of appreciation he makes with each mouthful have me sporting a semi, and I shift in my seat, trying not to make it obvious.

I excuse myself and take a moment to refresh in the loos, shooting off a quick text to my sister as I know how much she worries when I go on dates. When I return, Raz has a mischievous smile, and I'm tempted to check if I did my fly up.

"I've taken the liberty of requesting some of their cheesecake to go and the bill." His eyes twinkle as I sit down opposite him and finish my beer.

"Oh, really? And where were you thinking we could eat this cheesecake?" I ask my smile answering his as he bites his lip and hunger shines unmistakably in his eyes. *Oh, babe, we are not going to be having just a one-night stand, but I'll give you something to come back for.* My smile widens at that thought as the server comes over, and we split the bill, barely taking our eyes off of each other. The air around us crackles with promise as we take our boxed dessert and head out of the door.

Raz's flat is closer than mine, so we walk there. Our conversation is still easy and friendly but is now laced with an undercurrent of anticipation. I know what I want to do, but I wonder whether he thinks this will be a quick fling for one night. He has already touched on the subject of previous relationships, and they don't appear to be long-lived. I have no intention of fucking and running.

"Here we are," Raz states, pulling me from my thoughts as we enter a rather old looking building and make our way to the upstairs flat. This Victorian house would have once been owned by a middle-class family but is now separated into apartments. Raz's flat isn't messy but lived in, and there is a lingering smell of what I imagine is his body spray. It has a spicy undertone that makes me want to get closer to him so that I can smell it on his skin. *Don't rush*, I remind myself.

The light evening means that the lounge, where he has led me, is illuminated nicely in the evening sun. There is a two-seater sofa where I perch waiting as Raz disappears into the kitchen returning with the cheesecake on plates and a fork each.

"Want to watch a movie?" Raz asks, looking a little nervous now that we are sat here alone without the distraction of people around us. I'm reminded that he is younger than me and hasn't had that much experience either from the sounds of it.

"Yes, I'd like that. I don't know about you, but I'm not ready for this night to end." There I said it, nothing sexual about it, just that I want to spend more time with him.

"Me neither. Ben, I hope this doesn't sound weird, but you make me feel so comfortable, like I could talk to you about anything and you wouldn't judge me. I don't usually feel like that with anyone but Chlo." He avoids my eyes, looking down at the table as he covers his obvious embarrassment at being so open. His cheeks take on an adorable pink hue, and I wonder what else will bring out that colour in his face. I want to find out.

Setting my plate down on the side table next to the sofa, I leave my half-eaten cheesecake and focus on Raz. His knee bounces up and down as his fingers work over the controls flicking through films. His cheesecake sits untouched on the plate, resting on the side table on his side of the sofa. I rest my hand on his knee, and it stills. The muscle underneath my fingers tightens at my touch, and Raz stops flicking through the films. He turns towards me, assessing me with those pools of milky chocolate; his pupils dilate as I lean closer.

"I'm glad you feel comfortable with me, Raz." My voice has taken on a husky tone with the amount of restraint I am using to prevent myself from taking this too fast and ruining whatever it is we have blooming between us. Raz's left hand moves to my thigh as he faces me, and if it gets much higher, he will feel just how hard I am with thoughts of kissing him flooding my brain. Palming his jaw, I stroke at his soft skin, feeling the minutest amount of stubble under my thumb.

Our faces are close, breath mingling as Raz leans into me. I close the gap taking his lips first, slowly tasting him, testing that he wants this as much as I do. His eyelids flutter shut as he relinquishes control allowing me access to his mouth with my tongue. I meant to just have a taste, but I can't help myself taking the kiss deeper, pulling a moan from us both as this pull I have felt since I first met him threatens to drag me under with its intensity. I'm drowning in this man, and I don't want anyone to save me, not now, maybe not ever.

Chapter One

RAZ

Turning the tiny long-distance tracker over in my fingers, I let out a curse. I'd purchased this more high-end tracker to replace the rechargeable short-range one I'd originally placed in my best friend, Chloe's necklace. Back then, I thought the only reason to have one was to find the necklace if it got lost the same way her original one had.

"Stop torturing yourself with that thing." Ben's voice makes me jump a little. I hadn't heard him enter the room. He stands in the doorway, dressed in blue jeans and a T-shirt, his newly washed dark hair is styled in a way that would once upon a time have my hands itching to mess it up. His blue eyes are dark in this light as he looks at me with a mixture of concern and frustration.

"I know, I know... It's no good thinking about the what-ifs. But damn, Ben, it hurts when I think of how we could have found her sooner. Then she wouldn't have been..." I can't say the words. I still can't get the thought of Chloe's bloody and beaten body lying on that stinking mattress in the hovel of a basement out of my mind. That image won't leave me no matter how often I talk to her on Facetime and see her smiling.

"Raz, it's time. You need to move forward. Chloe is looking fantastic. At least she's still alive." Ben's voice trails off, and I turn to look at my boyfriend, seeing the worry and pain etched in the tiny creases by his eyes which he tries to hide. Sometimes I forget the tragedy that his family has recently endured, and then I feel guilty for wallowing in my own self-pity over the kidnapping and torture of my best friend. She's more than that, though. I love Chloe. I always have. But I'm not in love with her—not the way I am with this man in front of me, who, despite his own pain, has been shouldering mine as well.

"I'm sorry," I say, for what seems like the millionth time, and even to me, the words sound hollow. Strong arms circle me, pulling me against his familiar muscular chest, the one that, no matter how many times I touch and kiss, I can't seem to get enough of. His arms provide me with a safe haven when the darkness threatens to take hold.

"I know you are, but, Raz, it's been months now, and it kills me seeing you being so hard on yourself still." He pulls my head down onto his shoulder, and I go willingly. The only time I feel anything close to normal these days is in his arms. We stay like that for what seems like minutes but is likely mere seconds until he pulls away from me. The warmth of his hands on my face remind me I'm still alive, still breathing, at least I am, until his lips descend onto mine and take my breath away. My hands, which had rested on his waist, move to his hips, and as I attempt to pull Ben closer, he pulls away.

"I need to go over to Jen's. She's not in a good way, and that bitch Carl was shacked up with is causing a nuisance of herself." Ben walks towards our bedroom door, and I miss his heat instantly. To say our intimate relationship has suffered over the last few months is an understatement. Even our brief holiday away on Marcus' boat the *Sea Gem* when we moved Chloe's things down to Cornwall didn't resurrect our connection.

I had blamed that on the recent loss of his nephew and my dark moods over Chloe's abduction, and then her subsequent move to Cornwall. But, Ben and I still haven't regained the soul deep connection we once had. I am happy that Chloe is living with Marcus. In fact, I actively encouraged her to leave, but I find myself missing our coffees or the evenings when she would come over and have dinner with Ben and me. We'd play board games, something Ben and his family enjoy, and he brought with him to our relationship. Chloe and I soon became big fans too, having never had that sort of thing when we grew up.

I'm so lost in thought that I barely register Ben has left for his sister's already. Damn, I should have asked if he needed help. I pick the tracker up again and place it back in its case, throwing it into the top drawer of my bedside table. Giving myself a physical shake, I make my way downstairs, determined to get some work done and make the most of my time alone. I need to stop 'wallowing,' as Ben put it, and learn to move on. With that in mind, I text Ben and ask if he'd like a takeaway tonight. Maybe Jen would like to join us if she's up for it. My man has been there for me through thick and thin these last few months, and he's lost someone he loved, and despite his own pain, has still been holding me up.

My attempt to work leads to a lot of staring out of the window, so instead, I try unpicking the mess Ben's former brother-in-law has left Jen in. I manage a little research on what that bitch, Marilyn, Carl's big mistake, is entitled to. Not a lot, it turns out. The house they lived in is hers, but Carl was named on the mortgage and likely paying most of it. His life insurance policy should cover that, so in effect, Marilyn is mortgage free. Jen's house, however, Carl had let the insurance lapse, and it looks as though she will need to sell it. Not that she wants to stay there anyway. Jen has already made it clear that she can't live in that house anymore.

Marilyn seems to think she's entitled to half of that too. She isn't. The nasty piece of work had been hounding Carl to sell their family home because he was still paying the mortgage. The guy was in serious debt by all accounts, trying to make things right for Jen and their son while dealing with the mess that he got himself into by letting his dick stray. Now the bitch is claiming she's pregnant too.

Staring out the window into the back garden again, I realise I've been looking at the same thing on the screen for the last five minutes without really taking it in. So, I figure now is a good time as any to take a break and go out into the garden for a bit of fresh air. It's surprisingly warm outside despite it being October. I settle onto the bench seat with my slightly cool cup of coffee. I should probably have warmed that up again. Pulling out my phone, I notice a message from Ben, and my lips curl up into a smile as I think of him.

Ben: Takeaway is a good option. I'll see what Jen wants to do. Matt is here, and we are sorting through some of Jason's things. I don't know what time I'll be back, but I'll let you know when I leave, and then I can pick up the food on the way home.

I should have gone with him. Sorting out his dead nephew's belongings has got to be hard on all of them. I fire off a quick 'sounds good to me' text and breathe out loudly. Tears have already started to form in the corners of my eyes. *When did I become so emotional?*

Looking at my phone again, I realise I have a missed call from Chloe. I hadn't even noticed that my phone was on silent. Damn. Just seeing her name sends me into a bit of panic. Is she okay? *I'm being ridiculous—of course she's okay,* I tell myself. Dialling her number, I wait a few seconds before hearing her smiling voice on the other end. I can just picture her smiling at me, even if I can't see her.

"Hey you, I hope I didn't interrupt anything earlier." She laughs, a sound that tugs the corners of my mouth up into a wider smile, which feels foreign on my face. How long has it been since I actually smiled voluntarily, not the half-arsed attempts I make to appease the worry on Ben's face. As for laughing, fuck knows when I last laughed.

"No, I was working, and my phone was on silent. How are you?" It's a question I ask every time I speak to her, it's an automatic greeting almost, but I *need* to know she is okay.

"Great, thanks. I'm just off out on a Sea Safari with Marc. He's got the day off today. Hopefully, we will see some dolphins or seals." She sounds excited, and my heart swells a bit as I imagine her bouncing from foot to foot in anticipation of their adventure. "How's Ben doing?" she asks as she rustles with something down the phone.

"He's doing okay, I think. He's over at Jen's with Carl's brother Matt. They are sorting through Jason's stuff today." My hand runs through my hair as I realise I should really know how my boyfriend is doing. To me, he seems fine every day, but when was the last time we actually checked in with each other?

"That's rough. Is there anything we can do to help? I know we've been in our own little world here, but I think that both of us are finally starting to heal. So if there is anything we can do to help you two, please let me know." Chloe's voice is full of concern, and although it sounds silly, I am kind of relieved to hear it. She was emotionless for so long. It was as if the light inside her had gone out.

"I will, don't worry. I don't think there is much anyone can do right now. The whole family is grieving still. Being away on the *Sea Gem* for a week helped a bit, but it will take more than a week by the sea to heal that sort of hurt." I feel my own emotions starting to rise to the surface. Marc's voice sounds in the background, and Chloe quickly responds with an "Okay." Before I hear her shuffling about her end.

"Raz, I've got to go, but I want to hear how you are doing too. I'll give you a call soon, and we can have a proper catch-up. Give my love to Ben." I assure her I will as she puts the phone down, and the silence around me starts to press in. I need to get out. I feel as though I'm suffocating.

Grabbing my jacket and keys, I thrust my feet into a pair of trainers by the front door, lock the door and just walk, one foot in front of the other. Away from the house, away from my thoughts, away from my guilt. It's a constant companion these days, and Ben is correct. It is time that I do something about it.

Ben has two sisters and parents who listen. I have no one but Chloe, who isn't here and is dealing with her own healing, and Ben, who has his own grief to deal with. I see now how I haven't been allowing him to do that with my constant neediness. Not something I'm proud of. I don't know why today is the day that my mind starts to clear, but

I need to seize this opportunity and clarity to take action.

I find myself in a local park which isn't far from our house. It is one of the reasons we settled on this area to buy a place together, plenty of open space. Ben had been after getting a dog, but with us both out at work all day when we first moved in, that didn't seem responsible. Now though, I work from home mostly, and maybe a companion wouldn't be such a bad idea. I muse to myself as I enter the park gate and start walking along the concrete path which winds its way through the trees. I had been asked whether I would work for the police. There was a job there for me, but some of the ways I obtain my information aren't strictly orthodox, plus my contacts would stop helping me if I went 'all legal' on them.

When Chlo was found, I was in no fit state to consider their job offer, and it proved to me that I couldn't disassociate myself the way I wanted to. I need to follow digital trails and remain disconnected from the real people involved.

I've returned to freelancing, finding holes in companies' online security and sometimes finding people. The money I make more than pays for the bills. Ben's job also brings in a decent wage, so we do alright together, enough to be comfortable anyway. My thoughts are cut short by a dead weight hitting me from the side, which causes me to stumble. I'm barely able to stop myself from falling as a wet, slobbery tongue assaults me.

"Oh God, I'm so sorry. Are you okay? Duke doesn't realise not everyone needs a hug from him." The owner of the voice and likely the giant Great Dane, which is currently fussing about me for attention, comes into view through the trees—six foot, slim built, dark and handsome. Christ, the guy is gorgeous and looking at me with such concern that it takes my breath away. I nod my head, not just to free myself from those thoughts but to confirm that I am okay.

"It's fine. I wasn't paying much attention to my surroundings. He just took me by surprise." I play with the silky ears on the dog's head as he sits next to me, leaning heavily against my leg.

"Are you sure? Duke forgets he's the size of a human sometimes." Mr tall, dark, and handsome walks up to me and fastens a lead to Duke's collar.

"I'm fine, honestly. I probably just need more coffee to wake me up." Not sure why I said that. I'm not usually the type to start chatting to random good-looking men in a park, even if his dog is really gorgeous and overly friendly. Maybe he sensed my darkness and was hoping to shock it out of me with his body. A smile tugs at my lips at the ridiculous thought.

"My name's Charlie," Handsome says, extending his hand. I don't think Duke is the only one who has no idea of personal space. This guy is very close. So near to me now that I can see the interest in his deep brown eyes flare as he gives me a once over, no doubt attempting to assess if I'm damaged anywhere.

"Raz," I reply, allowing my hand to be clasped in his. A warm, comfortable sensation floods my body as his skin touches mine. I haven't felt that way for a while now. The only man whose touch has ever affected me like this is Ben. Thoughts of my boyfriend have me pulling my hand abruptly out of Charlie's. I let it drop to my side. *What on earth am I doing?*

"Well, if coffee is what you need, I was on my way to this great little food truck further along the path. They do amazing coffee and cake," Charlie says as he attempts to pull Duke away from my side. Before I can make up an excuse or even get my brain to work properly, he carries on, "I think Duke would like you to join us. If you aren't busy, that is? We don't want to intrude on your walk." The smile he gives me suggests that he's being truthful and, in fact, just being kind. I could be reading too much into this. "Please, let me buy you a coffee as a way to say sorry for Duke's brutish behaviour. It's the least we can do." He laughs as Duke licks my hand as if in agreement.

"Okay, coffee would be nice, but you don't need to buy me one. Honestly, he didn't hurt me, and really, I could do without being in my head so much." I scratch behind Duke's ears and look up again to find Charlie staring at me. He seems to snap out of it and pulls on the lead again. As I start to move, Duke moves with us, ambling along between us like a sleek fur-coated buffer. These feelings are a little foreign to me. Ben and I have been together for several years. He was my first steady boyfriend, the one person I felt truly knew me and understood who I was. When I met Ben, I was only nineteen, young, inexperienced and not capable of being openly in a gay relationship. He brought me out of myself, and taught me to love and accept who I am; even if I still find public shows of affection a little uncomfortable, I have come a long way with his love and support.

"So, do you live around here?" Charlie's friendly question draws my attention to the man walking beside me. It shouldn't put me on alert, but it does.

"Yeah, not too far," I hedge, unwilling to give away too much detail. After all, he may be good looking with a cute, rather large human-like dog, but I have no idea who this person is or if his bumping into me was a coincidence. My line of work attracts some shady sorts, *but no one should recognise me in person*, I reason with myself, trying to untie my stomach from the knots it seems to have found itself in. *What harm will it do to let him buy me a drink? He's only being friendly.* With that thought in mind, I quicken my pace to keep up with Duke and Charlie's long strides.

Chapter TWO

BEN

I feel bad for abandoning Raz like that, but the darkness that surrounds him threatens to engulf me sometimes, and I'm barely holding it together as it is. His text about food gives me little comfort; I've made the mistake before of thinking that we are turning a corner, only to have the weight of his guilt and the nightmares he constantly faces crash down on us, leaving me without the man I love.

When Chloe was here in Bristol, he would spend almost every day with her trying to coax her out of her shell. It became his mission to keep her from drowning. I understood. Of course, I did and helped in any way that I could, but once she left to go to Cornwall, it was like *his* light went out. They've always been close, so tight with each other that I thought at one point there might be more to it. Although once Raz let me in behind the walls he had built around himself because of his parents' complete rejection of his sexuality, I found out that there was nothing more than platonic love between the two of them. They were like very close siblings who told each other everything, and it wasn't long before I fell in love with her too. Chloe was so easy to be around, non-judgmental and fun, until that bastard took her and nearly destroyed not only her but everyone around her.

Marc had been a mess, and Raz was barely functioning, so it had been down to their friends and me to try and hold the pieces together. Then just when I thought we would all start to heal a little, my world was crushed. Raz had been in such a dark place, and it had been easier for me to take care of him than to allow the pain of my loss to take hold. Only now, I need a moment. I need to grieve and process what has happened to my family. To be there for my sister, who has lost her only child and is unable to get out of bed most days.

I look around what was once a happy family home and see only a shell. There is no light here anymore, either, no laughter.

The front door opening reminds me that I'm not alone in the house despite the silence. Elle, my other sister and the eldest of all three of us, bustles into the kitchen, where I have sought refuge from the heartache upstairs.

"How's it going here?" she asks quietly, nodding her head towards the upstairs rooms.

"Not easy, Elle. Jen isn't coping at all. Matt made her go and lie down while he cleared out Jas' room of all the trophies and stuff. I'm just taking a breath and getting everyone a drink. Do you want one?" I look towards my sister, an almost carbon copy of Jen with long dark hair and a curvy figure. There is no mistaking they are siblings. People say I look a lot like them too, but I don't see it myself. Yes, my hair is almost the same dark colour, but my eyes are slightly bluer and my features are more like Dad's, whereas Jen and Elle look exactly like Mum.

Elle and Jen are both a bit older than me. Mum and Dad hadn't planned on having a third child, so I was a 'happy occurrence,' as Mum puts it. I think that was something that Chloe and I gelled over, being the happy mistakes of our parents and the youngest of our siblings. Unlike Chlo, though, I'm fortunate; at least my sisters are alive, although Jen is barely hanging in there right now. I had to force her to shower when I arrived; the stench was awful.

"I'll have a coffee, thanks. I haven't had one since this morning. It's been mad at my house." She laughs, still keeping her voice down. None of us wants to raise our voices in this house anymore. I look behind her and realise a little late that she's on her own. Usually, one of her kids is with her.

"Where are the kids?" I ask as I pour her a mug of coffee.

"Jim's taken them to the cinema and then bowling. He wanted to give me time here on my own. The kids still don't understand or want to accept that Jason isn't here anymore." She lets out a small sigh, and I notice her hastily wipe what was likely a tear off her cheek as I turn and hand her the warm drink.

"You doing okay?" She looks at me, giving me the once over with her eyes. Both my sisters have always treated me with motherly affection, especially after I came out to Mum and Dad at sixteen.

"Yeah, I'm okay, Elle, just tired. It's been a long few months. Well, it's been a shit year really, and I just need something good, you know." I stop myself from saying too much. It's not like I'm the only one who has suffered a loss this year or who's been through hell.

"It's alright not to be okay, Ben. You don't have to be the one holding everyone up all the time." Her words are gentle as she walks over to me, putting her coffee down on the kitchen counter. In seconds I'm engulfed in a hug that I didn't realise I needed. I let myself breathe the familiar scent of family, of home. Patting my back, Elle moves away slightly but continues to stand in front of me. "You've lost your spark, Ben, and I know we have all been through the wringer recently, but you look so tired. Have you even told Raz how you feel?"

"He's not in a great place still, and I think the last thing on his mind right now is the future of our relationship. Raz is young, Elle."

She holds up her hand as if to stop me from going on, "He needs to know, Ben, and you both need to move forward. He isn't that young that he doesn't know what he wants out of life." Elle's voice is tinged with conviction, and I just know I'm in for an ear-bashing about my choices when creaking on the stairs draws her attention away from me. I try not to audibly sigh in relief. She isn't wrong, but the timing has been off; with everything that has been going on recently, it just doesn't feel right.

"Sorry to interrupt, but I need to bring these down and put them in the back of the car before Jen wakes up," Matt says as he brings a large box down the stairs in his arms. For a big man, he certainly can be quiet. I give him the once over, unable to help it. Matt is one fine specimen of a man; colourful tattoos litter the skin of his forearms. He looks tired with what appears to be day-old stubble gracing his face. I can appreciate a good-looking man when I see one, but that's as far as it goes. Plus, Matt is completely heterosexual and has a string of girlfriends who can attest to that. He may look a little rough, but he has a heart of gold, and as he spent a great deal of his time with his brother Carl and my sister, I know that big heart is just as broken as mine.

"How much more is there?" Elle asks as Matt places the box down on the kitchen counter briefly. He sighs as he takes a sip of the coffee I put in front of him.

"Jason's room is nearly empty apart from the bed and other big furniture. We've packed away all his personal belongings. There are still some of Carl's things in the spare room, though," he says as he lifts the box up again and heads to the door. Elle rushes in front of him to open it, and Matt nods his thanks as he passes through.

"He's taken Jas and Carl's death hard," Elle states the obvious, but I agree anyway. Haven't we all been blindsided by it. My thoughts are interrupted by movement on the stairs and the sound of a commotion outside. Jen must have woken up, and she hurries down the stairs faster than I've seen her move recently. Her hair is a mess of tangles, and her eyes are sunken and red, showing that she fell asleep crying again. Elle and I follow her out of the front door, just in time to see Matt pulling an irate woman away from the house.

"I have a right to look through any of Carl's things that she's kept here." The woman's voice is screeching as she fights against Matt's hold.

"There is nothing here that is any of your concern," Jen states, causing Matt and the woman, who seems familiar to me, to turn around. I move to Jen's side, pulling her against me with my arm around her shoulder. There is no way that spiteful looking hussy is getting near my sister.

"You need to go, Marilyn." Matt's voice is calm, but I can tell he is fighting back the anger that is written all over his face. Hearing the name, I now know who the woman is. Elle takes up position on Jen's other side, forming a united front. That bitch isn't coming anywhere near Jen or her house.

"You can't push me around, Matthew, not when I'm carrying your niece or nephew." Marilyn's shrill voice grates on my last nerve. Jen slumps against me, clearly unable to bear the scene unfolding in front of us.

"Take her inside," I instruct Elle as she gently removes Jen from my side and helps her indoors.

Matt continues to move Marilyn back to her car, hissing angrily at her as he does, "You can stop lying now, Marilyn. Carl was well aware of your bullshit. If you are even pregnant, it isn't Carl's."

"Of course, it's Carl's. How could you say such a thing!" Marilyn's tearful voice sounds fake. What the hell did my ex-brother-in-law ever see in her, and what is Matt talking about. Does he know something we don't?

"I think you know as well as I do. Carl told me, Marilyn. I know that he told you, so don't act innocent with me," he says as he opens her car door and practically throws her in the car's driving seat. "You've got all that you are going to get from my family. Don't come here again." Matt snarls at her. The look of shock on her face is priceless. I'm interested in getting to the bottom of this, but now is not the time. Matt looks like he wants to punch something as he turns around and slams the boot shut on his car.

"She has a nerve showing up here." Elle's voice startles me as she comes out of the front door.

"Where's Jen?" Matt asks. A look of concern takes over his face.

"Inside, I've got her a coffee and made her rest on the sofa. I think we should get that spare room sorted out now. This needs finishing. It's taking too much out of her." Elle leads the way back into the house, and I shut the door behind Matt, who walks ahead of me and immediately seeks out Jen.

Elle and I go back into the kitchen and collect the drinks. I hand Matt his as we all sit around the lounge focusing on Jen and Matt on the sofa. The moment feels monumental, as if something big is about to happen. "What's going on?" I look at Jen, who has tears pouring down her face again. Matt sits next to her and places an arm gently around Jen's shoulders.

Sipping my coffee, I take a moment to relish the warm, dark liquid. I only have a drop of milk in mine, so it's darker than everyone else's. Raz always says he could stand a spoon up in it. He prefers lattes and has to have tons of milk in his before he drinks it. I give myself an internal shake, trying to prevent my thoughts from straying or letting memories of happy mornings spent in bed with my boyfriend drinking coffee crowd my head. Those have become a thing of the past since Chloe's kidnapping. In fact, I can't remember the last time we laughed together.

Matt looks at Jen, who just seems to be staring into the coffee, which she has balanced on her knees between her two hands. "Jen?" I prompt, knowing there is something they both aren't sharing. Jen clears her throat and looks up at Matt.

"Are you sure?" she asks, looking at Matt, confusing me more. Matt nods and removes his arm but stays next to her on the sofa. The blue fabric looks somewhat faded, but I know having slept on it a couple of times recently that it is very comfortable despite its age and the cat hair.

Jen lets out an exhausted sigh and then directs her watery eyes at me. "It's about time you both knew, I guess." Elle leans forward in her chair, giving Jen her full attention, as do I, but my gaze drifts briefly to Matt, who isn't saying anything. The muscles on his forearms show how tightly he is holding his mug. I look back at Jen feeling confused at the tension in the room. Is she having an affair with Matt? They are very close, but my mind refuses to think that could be the case. Jen loved Carl. It broke her into a million pieces when her perfect life came crashing down that evening just over a year ago when Carl revealed that he had been shagging his work colleague. He even admitted it was a mistake but felt he should leave after letting Jen down so spectacularly. Marilyn had then persuaded him to move in with her. The rest, as they say, is history.

"Know what?" Elle asks as the silence stretches out in the room, and I feel my stomach knot as Jen appears to struggle with what she wants to say. "Just tell us, Jen. Is it about you and Matt?"

I guess I'm not the only one thinking they are awfully close. However, the surprised look from both of them suggests that we might be wrong.

"Me and Matt? No, what made you think something was going on between us?" Jen asks, looking confused. Matt just shakes his head. I'm pretty sure he is a little in love with my sister, even if she doesn't share those feelings, but he doesn't say anything.

"You seem rather close." I couldn't stop the words that formed in my head and left my lips without permission.

"We are. Carl and Matt were always close, as you know, and it has been that way with all three of us since I started dating Carl," Jen begins, and neither Elle nor I interrupt this time. It's clear Jen has something to get off her chest. "As you know, Carl and I tried for quite some time to start a family, but it just wasn't happening." Jen's eyes take on a faraway look as she remembers. I recall only too well the agonising months of them trying, and the look of utter defeat both Carl and Jen had on their faces almost all the time until she got pregnant with Jason. I'm not sure where she is going with this, and the look of confusion on Elle's face confirms she has no clue either. We stay silent.

"We never told anyone that we went to see a consultant. It turns out Carl wasn't able to have children. It's not something we could possibly have known. He was embarrassed and deeply concerned that Matt might have the same issue, so we agreed to let him know," she continues. The story is clearly taking its toll on her as I can see the slight tremor in her hand. Matt places a hand over hers, and she just nods as a silent communication between them happens, and he picks up the story.

"I went to the specialist myself and found that I was fine. Having had a few drunken conversations with Carl, I knew that he was trying to psych himself up to agreeing to get a sperm donor. So I offered mine," Matt says as a matter-of-fact, as Elle gasps, and the penny drops.

"Jason was my biological son."

Chapter THREE

RAZ

The guilt is back and not about Chloe this time. No, I've just spent the most enjoyable afternoon I've had in a long time with a man who is not my boyfriend. I guess that would be okay if he were just a friend, I don't have many close friends, but this was different. He was a stranger, and I can't deny that I found him attractive, not just because of his looks but because he didn't know me. He didn't know about my past or my failure where Chloe was concerned. Charlie didn't pry, didn't push me for information; instead, coffee turned into lunch at a nearby café, where we sat outside with Duke feeding him pieces of our sandwiches as we chatted about nothing important.

It turns out he is a nurse, working shifts at the Bristol Royal Infirmary. Today was his day off, and he wanted to spend it outside with Duke. So that's what we did. After lunch, we went back to the park, walked, played ball with

Duke, and chatted. Charlie is so easy to talk to; he put this down to his excellent bedside manner when I mentioned it, making me laugh, not just a little chuckle, God no, a full-belly laugh that got Duke all excited.

As I let myself into the quiet, dark house, I feel the guilt crawling all over me. *I haven't done anything wrong,* I remind myself. Spending the afternoon with another man walking his dog isn't being unfaithful, is it? I will just tell Ben about it. I'm sure he will be pleased that I got out of the house and enjoyed myself.

I try to busy myself, doing a little work, showering, tidying the already spotless house, but the wait is killing me. I haven't texted him, not wanting to come across as a needy boyfriend. I've done enough of that the last few months. I pick up my phone for the millionth time and put it down again, only to have a message ping up. It isn't from Ben.

Charlie: I had a lovely time this afternoon. Thank you for the chat and lunch. Maybe we can do it again sometime?

I look at the message twice. We exchanged numbers while we ate lunch. I guess I should have expected a text, but it still takes me by surprise, and I'm not sure how I feel about it.

The front door opening causes me to jump and drop my phone.

"Hey, sorry I'm so late. I grabbed your favourite from the Indian on the way back. Hope you're hungry?" Ben's voice drifts across to where I'm relaxing on the sofa, the TV on low, but I'm paying no attention to what's on. "You okay?" Ben stands behind the sofa, leans down and kisses me on the head, and I'm flooded with guilt again.

Jumping up, I follow him into the kitchen, wrapping my arms around his waist from behind as he unpacks the takeaway. "Yeah, fine. Just missed you." Something we often say to each other, but for some reason today, it feels false. I have missed him, but today I've had a distraction. Is that a bad thing? I kiss his cheek before letting go and bending to pull some plates out of the cupboard.

"How was it?" I ask when we are finally sitting at the kitchen table, takeaway boxes strewn between us as we share our usual favourites. I pull off a piece of my Peshwari naan and begin to chew whilst waiting for his answer. Ben looks preoccupied tonight; he's hardly said two words since he got in, which is very unlike him.

"Awful, it was so bloody sad. All those little things Jas collected. Bits of tat really, but they meant the world to him." Ben's voice breaks, and he stops eating. I reach over the table, feeling like a selfish bastard for being so caught up in my own shit that I haven't noticed the black circles under his eyes or how tightly wound he looks. Grasping his hand, I run my thumb over his fingers.

"I'm sorry, Ben. I should have been there with you." I feel sick to my stomach that I was out there enjoying myself this afternoon, and he was dealing with such heartbreak.

"How's Jen coping?" I try to get him to open up a bit more, knowing now that he's been keeping most of this to himself. I can see it written on his face. If this afternoon has given me anything, it's a bit more clarity on my life and how selfish I've been.

Ben's eyes are full of unshed tears as he looks at me across the table, "Jason wasn't Carl's son. Did you know?" His eyes narrow accusingly as I let go of his hand and let his question filter into my brain.

"What? What do you mean he wasn't Carl's son? There is no way Jen would have had an affair. She loved Carl!" *What on earth is he on about— did I know?*

"Did. You. Know?" Ben doesn't raise his voice, he never does, but still, the edge to his words cut me.

"Of course, I didn't, Ben. For fucks sake, you asked me to look into his financials, not his bloody medical history." I know my tone is a little harsh, but Ben has never looked at me like that before. If there is one thing we have always insisted on in our relationship, it's trust, which is likely why I'm feeling so shit about this afternoon. Only with this conversation blowing up the way it has, I don't feel like I can share how carefree and happy my afternoon was.

"Jason was Matt's son." Ben blows out a breath like he's been holding all this inside him and needs to just let it out.

"No way did Jen have an affair with Matt! I'm not buying it. You are joking, right?" It's an incredibly insensitive joke if it is one. Maybe he's trying to shock me out of my recent mood?

"She didn't have an affair. But yes, it's true. They told us today. Carl couldn't have children, so Matt offered to be a donor. They kept it to themselves." Ben looks lost and grabs a samosa, absentmindedly placing it into his mouth and chewing. Then he looks at me. Pretty sure my mouth is hanging open right now.

"Bloody hell!" *Nice one, Raz, understatement of the year. What can I say though?* That is one hell of a bomb to drop at the dinner table.

"You can say that again. Elle and I were gobsmacked and needed to leave so that we could digest it a bit. Matt has taken some stuff to the recycling centre and is staying on the sofa at Jen's tonight. So, I didn't ask her to join us," he says by way of an explanation. I hadn't even asked where she was, and again I feel guilty.

"Did you find out if that bitch is entitled to anything?" Ben asks as he tears off a corner of my naan. My lips try and jerk into a smile; he is always saying how he hates the coconut in the Peshwari naan but still ends up eating almost half of it. I relax a bit. This is normal. This is what our usual meals are like—sharing food and putting the world to rights. That must mean we are okay, right?

"Not much more than I already uncovered. She's not entitled to anything from Jen. That house is in Jen and Carl's name. Marilyn wasn't married to Carl, thank God, so she gets nothing but her own house paid off."

"Good. She turned up today—"

"At Jen's?" I ask, shocked at the audacity of the stupid woman.

"Yeah, luckily Matt intercepted her. She's a nutcase. Wanted to look through the stuff Carl had left at Jen's." Ben's eyes widen as he tells me this, indicating his disbelief at her behaviour.

"What on earth did Carl ever see in that woman?" This isn't the first time any of us have asked that question. Including Matt, who I know had quite a few choice words to say to Carl when his brother first revealed his infidelity. It kind of makes sense now why he would be so angry at Carl betraying Jen, if Jason was Matt's son.

"No idea, seriously. I just think he got caught up in the idea the grass might be greener, then found out quite quickly that it wasn't," Ben states as he finishes the last scrap of rice on his plate and puts his cutlery down.

"He moved in with her, though, and divorced Jen. Yet still spent an awful lot of time with Jen and Jas at their old house," I muse, finishing the last bit of my onion bhaji and pushing my plate away. My stomach feels strangely full for the first time in ages, reminding me that I'd had lunch out but also that I haven't been taking good care of myself recently.

"Jen says Carl wanted to come back to her. Even after all that they went through he still loved her. He was the one who asked for a divorce as he felt he betrayed her trust. I think the guy was just seriously confused." Ben looks at my empty plate and smiles but says nothing about it.

"Confused or not, he shouldn't have had an affair in the first place. Jen did everything for that man, and it's obvious they really loved each other. Let's be honest, he was an idiot." I stretch my arms above my head and feel the T-shirt I'm wearing ride up a little. Ben's gaze goes straight to my exposed skin, his eyes flaring with lust that I've not seen for a while, or maybe it's been there all this time, and I'm only just noticing it. I decide to try my luck. I'm done being a shit boyfriend.

"Keep looking at me like that, baby, and I'm going to have to cut our conversation short." I lace my words with all the pent-up emotions my body is finally starting to feel today. Focusing my attention solely on the gorgeous man in front of me as he cocks an eyebrow at me. *That's right; you know what I mean.* My lips curl up as I take a sip from the glass of water I've barely touched throughout our meal. Licking my lips slightly, my body heats as Ben tracks the motion with his eyes. I'm filled with an overwhelming need to take his worries away, even if it's just temporarily.

Ben looks unsure but curious, and I remember that we've been here before over the last few months. Occasionally I would drag myself out of the fog and want to feel something, only to find that both of us were not in the right place mentally or physically to take things further. I'm not the only one who has been suffering here, and it's damn time I remember that. He starts to get up from the table, ready to clear things away, obviously thinking it's best not to push. Does he even understand that I want him right now? How long is it since I took his cock in my mouth and showed him just how much I love him? Fucked if I can remember.

I grab his wrist, not even caring that I'm not being gentle because I know my man likes it a little rough sometimes. That's the beauty of being in a long-term relationship, or so I've discovered, knowing each other well enough to know when to go slow, or like now, when to move fast. I don't want to give him a second to come up with an excuse. This is happening, right here, right now.

"Raz?"

I hate that uncertainty in his voice; it was never there before. He would have been unzipping his fly by now, knowing exactly where this was going.

"Ben…" I run my tongue over his name in my mouth, feeling the length of time it has been absent like a knife to my chest.

Getting up from my chair, I step into his space, crowding him so that his back hits the edge of the table. I still have hold of his wrist, holding it down on top of the table. We are almost the same height, with me being just a few inches taller and, especially now, leaner. His blue eyes swirl with emotion as he looks into mine. Ben's breath hitches as I use my other hand to stroke his cheek. His eyelids close briefly as he leans into my touch—God, I've missed this feeling.

We don't need words or conversations; we've danced this dance before, all we need right now is to feel. I run my fingers over his newly acquired stubble, loving the rough texture against my fingertips. Grasping the back of his neck, I slam my mouth onto his. Our kiss is messy, filled with pent-up need. His moan has me pulling his body closer until the only thing between us is a layer of clothes. My hand leaves his wrist and lays claim to his hip, pulling him against my hard-on, wanting him to feel what he still does to me. A satisfied noise leaves me, swallowed by our kiss, as I feel his hard length rub mine through our jeans.

"Fuck, Raz. I've missed you." Ben's words are whispered against my lips as he pulls back, his breath coming out in short bursts.

"I've missed me too," I admit as I grind against him. It's not enough. I need to show him just how much.

I drop down to my knees in front of him, undoing his jeans in a rush of fumbling fingers to pull them down his hips, taking his boxer shorts with them. There's no time for going slow, and I have a feeling neither of us is in the mood for romantic right now. My frantic movements draw a moan from Ben as he looks down at me with hooded eyes filled with love and lust. His hard length juts out at my eye level, and it's all I can do to stop myself from drooling. My own hard shaft pulses painfully against the zipper of my tight jeans.

"Are you hard for me, baby?" he asks, his tone showing signs of strain as I grip his cock in my hand, pumping it slowly. "Show me," he demands, and I comply. Standing up briefly to unzip my jeans, I let my cock escape as I pull my jeans and boxers down to my thighs. Before I can lower myself to my knees again, Ben reaches out and grips my cock tightly, knowing how I like it. His lips crash into mine furiously, demanding I show him just how much I need him. This side of Ben is mine; no one else sees him lose control the way I do. His tight grip on my shaft starts a rhythm I know will have me coming in minutes. He thumbs the pre-cum from my slit, moaning his approval into my mouth as our tongues battle for dominance.

It's been too fucking long since I've felt this, the all-consuming passion that only Ben has ever made me feel. I pull back breathless, running my hand down his chest as he continues to pump me leisurely, with just enough speed and grip to make me beg him to fuck me, but that is not what is happening here. No, I feel a desperate need to show him how much he means to me. A growl escapes him as I pull back completely; the look of frustration on his face almost makes me smirk. It's soon replaced as I drop to my knees again, taking the blunt head of his leaking member into my mouth. Sucking hard. Ben lets out a delicious hiss, then groans, his fingers finding purchase in my hair. One hand holds tight to the table behind him, and the other has a loose grip on my head as he allows me to take over.

I relish the feel of his hardness inside my mouth. Using my tongue along the underside, I worship him with my mouth, sucking the way I know he loves as I move my head, increasing the pace, wanting him to lose control.

My own cock leaks with need, but as I go to wrap my hand around it, hoping to relieve the pressure, Ben grabs my hair, forcing my eyes up to his. "Don't fucking touch yourself. That cock is mine." That's what I've been missing, the connection we have is like nothing I've ever known. His dominant behaviour, which I never knew I wanted until I met him, has been missing for so many months now as he has tried to care for not only me but his sister as our worlds fell apart. Not once has he forced himself on me, and even when we tried to be intimate, it was loving but tame when we managed it at all. This, this is what I need.

Ben's hips start to move as he seeks a release I know is coming as his thighs clench. I grip them tightly, holding on as he takes over, grunting his need and hammering into my mouth like a man possessed. I breathe through my nose, desperately turned on as his pace increases, and I can't catch a breath.

"Fuck. Raz. Oh, Fuck!" Ben yells as he comes down my throat; hot streams of cum coat my tongue as I suck and swallow everything he has to give me. Feeling like I am home finally after a long period of time away. I'm so close to coming myself, it's painful. My knees click slightly as I stand up and find myself immediately hauled against a strong, hard chest. Lips find mine claiming me. I'm so lost in the feeling of this man that I almost don't notice as he spins me around. My lower back is pushed up against the table.

"Keep your hands on the table, Raz," he orders, sinking to his knees in front of me. A moan leaves my lips as I fight the need to run my hands through his hair. My fingers grip the edge of the table behind me as Ben pushes my clothing further out of the way. My legs are now bound with the tight jeans holding my thighs in place, making me wish I could kick them off.

"Ben, I need you."

Chapter FOUR

BEN

I've been longing to hear those words for months now. They spill from his lips in desperation as Raz thrusts his hips forward, almost mindless with desire. This is how I want him. It's like a fog has been lifted, and his dark expressive eyes are finally showing me how he feels.

I'm not going to make him wait, not when it's taken us this long to get back here. I don't know why today is different, but I'm not going to waste a moment second-guessing it. Gripping the base of his cock I take him in my mouth. The moan that comes from above me has blood rushing to my barely softening cock. It's been so long since we've had this type of desperate need for each other that I'm almost ready for round two.

"Yes, baby. Yes, like that." His words leave his lips on panted breath as I lick and tease. Finally relenting, I suck his throbbing length, noticing with joy the white knuckles on his hands as he does what I asked of him and holds tight to the table. I know, looking up at his face as I bob my head over and over again, taking his hard cock into my throat, just how much he wants to grab ahold of my head and pound into me. His legs shake and quiver as I run my hands up the back of his thighs; taking hold of them, I set a punishing pace.

"Oh fuck, Ben, don't stop, baby, please, I need…"

Oh, I know exactly what you need, my love. Hollowing my cheeks, I suck harder, demanding that he comes with my mouth and the tight punishing grip of my fingers on his legs. I hold him still, keeping him in place, showing him I own his pleasure just the way I have always done. He is mine and always will be.

Salty cum sprays the back of my throat, and I hastily swallow. Licking and pumping his length as he jerks his hips, then sags against the table, his taut jaw finally relaxes in a way that has been missing for such a long time. Raz extends his hands which I take, feeling the soft skin against mine as he pulls me to my feet. We stand there in front of each other, our clothes hanging half off and wrinkled. Our breathing is unsteady as we just stare at each other. I'm scared that he will shut down again, even after all of that emotion, so I reach out, touching his face. Raz's eyes momentarily close as he leans into my touch. I step closer, wanting to reduce the gap between us even though it is barely there.

Although we are practically the same height, I now have a couple of inches on Raz as he sags against the table, his legs out at an angle in front of him; he looks relaxed. Dark eyes seek me out, and he seems about to say something, but I need to say this. I place a finger over his lips, and his eyes dance with amusement.

"I've missed you, Raz. So damn much."

The amusement is replaced with an expression that looks both sad and guilty, so I rush on, not wanting him to feel that I'm blaming him.

"I know we have both had so much to deal with, and things have been really tough. I just want us to get back what we had. I know it will take a while, but...."

"We will, Ben. We will. I promise. From now on, I'll make more of an effort. I'm so sorry that I've shut you out."

Raz reaches out and pulls me against him. We stay like that for goodness knows how long, just breathing each other in as I reassure him that it wasn't just him. Then he starts to laugh and eases me away slightly. My confusion must show on my face as I step back a little, not wanting to crowd him.

"Look at the two of us, clothes all over the place. Let's clear up in here, go upstairs and watch something on the TV in the bedroom?"

He asks the last part as a question, but I'm already nodding my head and pulling up my jeans and boxers. I don't want this to end.

Showering took a little longer than expected. It felt like we were renewing our claim on each other as we soaped and washed, exploring every muscle, every inch of the other's body. Now, as I watch him towel his hair as he strolls into the room, a pair of checked pyjama trousers hanging low on his hips, I feel the same sense of belonging as I always do when I see this man of mine. It's on the tip of my tongue to ask him, but I can't… not yet. The timing is all wrong, and we have only just started to mend what was broken between us.

Raz puts the towel over the radiator. Recently he has been just leaving them in a pile on the floor. He shrugs his shoulders, giving me an apologetic smile, "I know I've been a slob."

"It wasn't that bad, babe, but thank you for not leaving it on the floor." He knows how it grates on me, and honestly, I haven't been in a good place either, so the last thing I needed was to clear up after him. I did though.

"What are we watching?" he asks, climbing across our double bed and pulling back the duvet. His warm body close to mine distracts me momentarily as he pulls the pillows up behind him so he can lean against the headboard next to me. Raz always runs a little hotter than me, so he sleeps in just his pyjama bottoms or boxers in the summer. I prefer to wear a T-shirt as well, especially now as I've piled on a couple of pounds in the last few months, so I'm not quite as confident about my body. I search for something light to watch before we sleep, but now I can't drag my eyes away from his tanned torso.

"Ben?" Raz nudges me with his shoulder. I realise I've just been staring and snap out of it. It feels like my libido has woken up, and now there is no calming it down. I laugh internally at my ridiculous thoughts—plenty of time for that. I hand him the remote, not really that interested in the telly anymore. I just want to spend time with my man.

"You choose. I'll get us a glass of water each, so we don't have to go back downstairs again," I say as I reluctantly leave the warm cocoon of our bed, sliding on my slippers to prevent my feet from getting cold on the hard-wood floor downstairs.

"Okay, maybe bring up that cheesecake I saw you hide in the fridge earlier?" He laughs, turning his attention to the television on the wall. My lips lift in a smile; if there is one thing I know guaranteed to lift Raz's spirits, it's a dessert. He loves cakes and puddings, and they never seem to affect his body either. Then again, he does work out at home in the spare room and loves to walk. Me, I'm not so keen on the weights and high impact stuff he usually does, but I don't mind a good walk or a bit of yoga. I make a note to myself to start that again.

Everything has been so up in the air, especially as I've been helping Jen with the house. I need to make more time for myself and get back into a routine again. Work has become busy, and to be fair, I've lost interest in my job. It hasn't been fulfilling for quite some time. The projects I manage together with a team of colleagues are still just as mentally challenging as they ever were but with the increase in responsibilities within my team and the stress that comes with that, plus all that has happened in my private life, I'm beginning to doubt my long-term commitment there. It is something I need to discuss with Raz. His work can be done remotely from anywhere, and I know how much he misses Chloe, I do too, but also I miss Cornwall. I didn't think I could become attached to another place so quickly, but I did. I love the slower pace of life and the beaches. My only worry is leaving Jen behind, but I know she has our parents and Elle. Plus, Jen would be the first to tell me to grab life by the balls and make the most of it.

I flick on the light downstairs as I step off the bottom stair, it wouldn't do to trip over, and it's certainly getting dark early at night now. Autumn has fully arrived, bringing a chill in the air and the promise of crisp wintery mornings. I imagine what the coast will be like in the winter, less busy no doubt, but the sea will still be beautiful. A glow draws my attention, and I realise that we've left our phones down here in our haste to get upstairs.

Checking the doors are definitely locked, I pull the box with two slices of cheesecake out of the fridge and grab a couple of plates and forks. Setting them down on the kitchen island temporarily so that I could pick up our phones and put them in the pockets of my pyjama trousers to take upstairs. Raz's phone glows again, and as I pick it up, I see he has two messages. Glancing at it quickly in case it's from Chloe. I see the name, Charlie.

Charlie: You don't have to reply, but I'd

like to see you again...

The rest of the message isn't on the screen, and I can't open it without Raz knowing I've looked at his messages. A sick feeling settles in my stomach. Who is Charlie? I've not heard that name before, and Raz only has a few close friends. I try not to read too much into the fact he hasn't mentioned meeting up with anyone. After all, maybe it was just someone who needed a job done. *Don't let your insecurities take a hold, Ben,* I remind myself. Raz and I have no secrets from each other; we have always been clear about that. No matter how difficult, we have always discussed everything, never shying away from tough subjects. *Until he shut himself off,* an unhelpful voice in my head niggles at me, trying to place doubt in my mind.

I thrust the phone into my left pocket and put my own in the right, briefly making sure I hadn't got any messages from Jen. Then shaking my head slightly to rid it of any negative thoughts, I try to concentrate on the night ahead with my boyfriend, who is waiting upstairs, half-naked. Yeah, that ship has sailed. My libido has taken a hike. I pick up the plates and forks, and head up the stairs hoping that it will return before the evening is over.

"Raz, I picked up your phone..." My words die as I enter the room to find him stretched out on the bed, remote still in his hand with a romcom on pause on the telly, fast asleep. I contemplate waking him up for the cheesecake he wanted but instead, noticing the dark circles under his eyes and remembering the nightmares which have been a frequent visitor every night, I turn around and take the dessert back to the refrigerator. I guess the night is over now. We could both do with some more sleep, I reason with myself and try not to be disappointed.

Returning to our room, I shut off the telly, plunging the room into darkness and try to slide under the duvet next to him without waking him up. Raz stirs a little bit, but as I pull his body against mine, wrapping my arm around his chest, spooning him from behind, he settles again. I lie in the dark, listening to his even breathing, trying to calm my thoughts so I, too, can fall asleep. However, my mind is not having any of it. It conjures a younger, fitter man who loves to work out and spend evenings in the clubs dancing, someone who would pull Raz out of himself. I see Raz laughing and joking again the way he used to, and my thoughts spiral out of control. My breathing picks up, and even though I have the man in question in my arms, I can't stop the doubt from creeping in. I know that the lack of sleep and our relationship taking a hit with the recent trauma is playing a considerable part in these crazy thoughts, but they won't go away.

Knowing that I'll end up waking Raz if I start to fidget as my mind goes over the possibility that my boyfriend may be cheating before I've even got a chance to get my facts straight. I get out of bed slowly. Making sure to tuck the duvet around him so that he doesn't feel the absence of my warmth. I know I'm being ridiculous. I've never doubted Raz before; we've always been open about our feelings for one another. Even if he doesn't like public displays of affection, he is or rather was, very loving when we were alone.

I pick up my phone from its charging point on my bedside table and head downstairs. I may as well read in the lounge and maybe look at job opportunities down in Cornwall to push my mind past the present and into the future. *A future that I intend to spend with Raz*, I remind my whirling thoughts as they thrust ridiculous scenarios at me.

Chapter FIVE

RAZ

Ben isn't in bed when I wake up coated in sweat from yet another nightmare. I feel his absence immediately. Reaching over to his side under the duvet, I find it cold. *Where is he? It's still dark outside.* I turn towards my bedside cabinet and find my phone on the charging dock. Fumbling around, I manage to sit up and take note of the time. It's only two in the morning. Fear sits in my stomach still, remnants of the same nightmare I've been having since we discovered Chloe in the basement of that derelict house. Every time she was dead, we didn't get there in time to save her.

Needing to get away from my dream and dispel this fear that something has happened to Ben or that he's left, another recurring nightmare. In this one, he gets tired of my shit and finds someone more mature to settle down with. I get up and pad on bare feet, wishing I'd had the energy to find my slippers because it's damn cold on this floor downstairs. The side lights in the lounge are on, giving the otherwise dark room a warm glow. My lips curl up a little at the sight of Ben, eyes closed, with his Kindle resting on his chest, lying on the sofa. He looks so peaceful. I pull the blanket off the back of the chair and cover him gently, not wanting to wake him. Then return to our empty bed upstairs, wondering what caused him to take himself off downstairs in the first place.

I pick up my phone as I get into bed, knowing it will be a while before I go back to sleep again. I may as well answer Charlie's messages.

Raz: It was nice to meet you and Duke today. Thank you for lunch. It would be great to meet up with you again soon.

Three little dots appear just as I'm putting my phone down. That's strange. It's two in the morning.

Charlie: Hi there, I thought you might be ignoring me.

He ends his text with a laughing emoji. Talking to him today had been so easy, with no drama or prior trauma to work through. Just two people getting along and chatting. Although, if I'm honest, I did most of the talking. Charlie just listened.

Raz: What are you doing up at two in the morning?

Charlie: I could ask you the same thing. I'm working the phones tonight.

Raz: I'll let you go. I woke up and saw your message. Thought I'd reply as I was awake.

Charlie: Good job my phone is on silent all the time then.

More laughing emojis pull a small chuckle from my lips.

"What you laughing at in the dark, babe?"

Ben's voice startles me so much I drop my phone on the bed. Reaching for it, I turn it off and place it back on charge. Wondering why I feel guilt rolling around in my stomach.

"Just a funny meme." *Why the hell am I lying?* Honestly, though, I don't want to talk about Charlie in the middle of the night with my boyfriend, who has obviously got something on his mind, or he wouldn't have been sleeping downstairs.

"Hmmm." His response is less than convincing. Maybe we should have that talk now. I won't have him thinking I'm doing anything underhand.

"Ben—"

"No, sorry, it's me. I'm tired and grumpy. Forget it. Did you have a nightmare?" His voice sounds full of concern, and the churning guilt inside me increases.

"Just the same as usual. What about you?" I ask as he pulls back the duvet and slides in next to me.

"I couldn't sleep. A lot on my mind, I guess. Thought I'd read that book you suggested the other day." He pulls me over, and I go willingly, resting my head on his chest.

"*All the Cuts and Scars We Hide* by Garry Michael?" I question, feeling his reply as well as hearing it.

"Yes, it's amazing."

I smile. I knew he would love it. My paperback version is getting a little dog eared where I've reread it a couple of times.

"I knew you'd like it, even if it's a little different to your usual reads." I chuckle, knowing Ben's preference for dark romance.

"It's excellent. You were right. I'll take a look at his other books next. What was that other author you wanted me to try?" he asks, and the conversation feels light and comfortable.

"Michael Robert," I answer, excited that he is finally getting around to reading the authors I suggested a while ago. Before everything went dark, before the chasm between us widened so much that I began to wonder if we would ever bridge it.

"Yes, that's the one," he replies, sounding sleepy but content. I snuggle into him, loving the feel of his body against mine. There are no empty sheets between us as there have been on numerous occasions recently as we both battle our demons alone in the dark.

"Sleep, baby," I whisper as his breathing becomes more spaced out, and the hand that was rubbing unconsciously at my arm whilst he held me against him stops then starts again, only to stop a minute later and go still.

-

Cracking my eyes open, I sigh in relief, seeing the tiny amount of light spilling underneath the curtain. I slept for the rest of the night, thank goodness. I don't remember dreaming again, which is a plus. As I roll over, I'm immediately aware of the space next to me. Pushing my hand out, I touch the sheet—cold again. Ben must have got up already. The smell of shower gel finally registers from the slightly open doorway of our ensuite. I pull myself up to a more vertical position, stretching my arms over my head and feeling my muscles complain.

Throwing back the covers, I pull my protesting body out of bed and head off to take care of my personal needs in the small bathroom. The shower is still covered in water droplets, and steam hangs in the air. Brushing the condensation off the mirror with a swipe of my hand, I peer at a distorted version of myself in the fogged glass. The stubble on my face hints at weeks of neglect, and I could certainly do with a haircut. I ignore the dark circles under my eyes, evidence of my sleepless nights. Once I'm in the shower, I let my mind wander over the events of last night. Feeling that loved and close to Ben again felt like coming home. Having him taking control like that again, not treating me like I might break at any minute, was something that, in my darkened state, I hadn't even realised I'd been missing. I try to ignore the hardening between my legs and wash quickly to get out of there. For some reason, taking care of myself doesn't feel right. There is only one person's hands I want on me at the moment, and he's likely at work already.

"I brought you a cup of tea. It's on your bedside cabinet." Ben's voice scares the crap out of me as I leave the ensuite in nothing but a towel around my waist.

"Bloody hell, Ben! I thought you'd gone to work," I exclaim, trying to calm my racing heart with a few deep breaths. My hand, which had flown to my chest of its own accord, starts to lower. There is no answering smirk from my boyfriend, no laughter at my expense, just a look of hurt that flits across his face before he shuts it down and his features turn blank. He's looking at me but not really seeing me.

"I've got to go. Just thought I'd bring you a drink up." Ben's voice is monotone, lacking his usual emotion.

"What's the matter?" I ask, wondering if I've managed to do something wrong without knowing about it. I've been in such a fog until yesterday when it started to lift a little. I try not to focus on how much talking to Charlie helped with that.

"Nothing. I'm just late. I'll see you later." He turns and walks out of the bedroom door and down the stairs without so much as a touch or a kiss goodbye, leaving me stunned at the sudden change in his demeanour. What the hell happened?

I hear the front door slam, and it vibrates through my

body, bringing tears to my eyes, which I quickly wipe away. *Men don't cry*, my father's voice reminds me in my head, sounding just as angry and disappointed in me as he always was. It's been a while since I let him get into my head, and years of discussions with Chloe and Ben before I felt that what he said about me wasn't justified or correct. My father was a strict man. Originally from Israel, he settled here, having met my mother on her pilgrimage to Jerusalem. Chloe always said she was shocked at how different I was from my fanatically religious parents.

All my life, I hadn't fitted in. Unlike my brothers and sisters, who I no longer see, I was always the black sheep of the family. Now I am shunned, a shame to them all for openly admitting to being gay and, worse still, living with my boyfriend. My father refused to even look at me, let alone talk to me after he found out, and that carried on until he died. I thought that maybe my mum or even one of my brothers or sisters would try and reach out afterwards, but they didn't. I have learned to accept that I am effectively an orphan.

Chloe was always there, my saviour, my best friend, and confidant when things got dark. Then I met Ben, and although I struggled with my feelings towards him which were so strong from the beginning, I finally felt that I had another ally in this world. That I finally had a family. Now though, I'm wondering if I might have lost this family as well.

I know that Chloe isn't really lost, she is putting her

own life together in Cornwall with Marcus, and I can't fault them for what they have found together. But my relationship with Ben has been strained over the last few months; understandably, after all that we have been through. I could kick myself, though, for burying myself inside and not reaching out as I should have. To share my feelings, my darkness, my grief and guilt with the one person who understands me and who I know deep down wouldn't judge me. Instead, I've wallowed, leaving him to battle his own grief, which far outweighs mine. At least Chloe is still alive.

Walking slowly, lost in thought, I make my way over to my side of the bed and sit down on the unmade sheets. The mattress dips as I reach absentmindedly for the mug placed on my bedside cabinet. It's full of hot tea, and I press my lips together, blowing the steam from the top before taking a sip. My phone's screen lights up with a message. Placing the steaming cup back down, I reach for it before it goes dark.

`Charlie: Just getting home. It was a busy night. Your text was a light relief.`

`Charlie: Do you fancy a coffee later this afternoon?`

I look at the messages, the first one must have come in whilst I was in the shower. I contemplate my reply. Should I meet up with Charlie? I've only just met him, but he is easy to talk to and be with. We are only friends, and that's okay, isn't it?

Then why haven't you told Ben? my inner voice criticizes me.

Chapter Six

BEN

Am I just being overly sensitive? There is probably a reasonable explanation for this person to be texting Raz. The message said they texted last night. When last night? Before or after he had his mouth on my cock and made me feel like we were connecting again?

I know I shouldn't have looked, but the message lit up the screen like a beacon in the darkened room as I placed the tea I'd made him down on his bedside cabinet. It's work, right? Why am I second-guessing this? Raz and I are strong. I wouldn't be contemplating asking him to marry me if I didn't think we were forever. You could say the realisation that life is too short and can be taken away from you at any point did have something to do with me wanting to take this next step, and I'm well aware of how spooked Raz might get. It took a long time for him to be comfortable with our relationship after the mindfuck that is his family, but I thought that we had moved past that now, well before our worlds turned upside down we had.

Deciding that I need another person's input and just a bit of reassurance, I activate the voice control in my car and, after a few attempts manage to get it to call my sister Elle, who I know will be awake with her kids at this time in the morning.

"Hey, Ben. Everything okay?" Elle's voice sounds loud in the car, and the background noise of her children pulls a smile to my lips as I turn down the volume.

"Is it a bad time?" I ask as she yells at my nephew to clean his teeth. In my mind, I can visualise her standing at the bottom of their stairs, shouting up to the kids to get ready for school.

"It's always a bad time." Elle laughs. "No, go on. What did you ring for?"

"I don't know, Elle. It's stupid really." I wonder whether I should have rung her. It seems so trivial now when I try to voice my concerns as I navigate the busy Bristol roads on my way to work.

"Well, it's something, Ben. You wouldn't have rung this early in the morning if it wasn't. Are you on your way to work?" she asks, then the line goes muffled as she asks my niece if she's brushed her hair.

"Yes. Look, I shouldn't have called. I'm just being stupid. I'll speak to you soon, Elle. You're busy, sorry." I check the road is clear twice before leaving the junction.

"Ben, you know you can talk to me at any time. I'm here for you. How about I meet you for lunch today? I'm coming into town even though it's my day off. I need to get some socks for Beth. Goodness knows what she does with them." Elle's laugh tapers off as she reassures her daughter that it is just me she is talking to and not some random stranger. I can't help the laugh that escapes me as I hear Beth moaning at her mum.

"That would be great, yes. Text me about twelve-ish and let me know where you are," I say as Elle agrees, then ends the call.

Just hearing my sister's no-nonsense voice calmed my mind. I'm glad that we are meeting at lunch. There is a lot to discuss, including the bombshell Jen and Matt dropped yesterday. Because Carl and Matt were so similar in features, if not in build, I would never have twigged that Jas wasn't Carl's. They had the same eyes, but many of Jason's features and mannerisms came from Jen.

I scour the car park for a space, humming my satisfaction when I find one and reverse into it quickly. A ping on my phone has me checking my notifications as I pull my coat on and get out of the car. Locking it up, I sling the strap of my messenger bag over my head so it crosses my body, and then I leave the car park. The notification is from an employment site I joined recently in my need to move my life forward and stop feeling like I am drowning in the present. There are jobs that meet my criteria, according to the message. I start to scroll as I enter the lift paying no attention to the occupants. More faceless people working the same hours in the same building. Some work for the same company, but a simple nod is all we manage at this time in the morning, all lost in thought or scrolling through our phones.

There are a few jobs that might hold some promise and a lot that have nothing to do with the specifications I added to my search for employment in Cornwall. I need something that will at least be the same sort of wage, if not higher, and only two meet that requirement. Still, I send off my CV and pocket my phone as I approach my desk. I'm lucky mine is by the window and not in the middle of the open-plan office. But as I look around, seeing a few heads bent over their desks already, I know that even with a window seat, this job is no longer for me. I feel trapped and in need of a change.

The view over the rooftops of the nearby buildings isn't too bad, I can still see the sky, which holds the promise of a dry day, but I find myself aching to see the ocean again. I don't kid myself into thinking I would find work overlooking the sea, but maybe knowing that my journey home would take me through the windy country lanes instead of the heavy, stationary traffic in this city would lift my spirits no end.

Logging onto our internal system, I put my coat over the back of my chair and the bag on the floor under my desk. I nod a greeting to several of my co-workers as I wander towards the kitchen to make a coffee before getting sucked into work. The bright fluorescent lights of the kitchen are a stark contrast to the gloomy interior of the office. Everything is bright and white here, giving off a false sense of cleanliness. I locate my mug in the dishwasher and fill the kettle, still lost in my thoughts about Jen's revelations and Raz's messages from *Charlie*. I don't know why this is affecting me so much. Raz doesn't have many friends, and I know all of them, if not closely, certainly by name. I shake my head slightly as the kettle boils, trying to dislodge this feeling of insecurity which just isn't normal for me.

"Ben, do you have a minute?" The tired voice of my boss sounds from behind me, pulling me out of my thoughts. I guess coffee will have to wait.

The rest of the morning is a blur of phone calls and paperwork, staring at the computer, trying to make sense of what I see on the screen whilst constantly being asked to help one of my colleagues or my boss. By lunch, I'm frazzled, and it's very tempting to blow Elle off and just sit at my desk with a sandwich. However, I pull on my coat and tap my pockets, ensuring I have my wallet and phone before joining a few of my workmates in the lift. The trip down to the reception involves more talk about work, but at least it's brief, and I make my excuses as I leave them chatting and walk away in the direction of Cabot Circus, Bristol's big shopping centre.

Taking a good inhale, I breathe in the cold air. Winter

is creeping up on us, with the nights getting darker earlier and the mornings dark when I get up. If I spent all day in the office, I wouldn't see any proper daylight, just the early morning sun rising as I leave the house and make my way to work. One of the many reasons I need a better work-life balance. Raz is now working from home, and I feel we could do with seeing more of each other. With his work, we could be based anywhere in the world, but I think being near the sea and, for Raz, near Chloe is the right move for us now. I just know my family would love somewhere they could come and stay, they all love coastal holidays, and Jen used to spend a lot of time in Cornwall with Carl before they split, as that's where he grew up. His dad still lives in Pendlebrook, which I think is far too much of a coincidence, and more likely fate telling me that there might be a life to be found in that tiny town by the sea.

Elle is waiting for me outside the cinema, checking her phone and then looking around. A huge smile lights up her face when she spots me, pulling an answering one from my lips.

"Hey, sis," I pull her into my arms for a hug. She might be older than me, but her petite five-foot frame is dwarfed in my embrace.

"Oomph, get off, you oaf, I'm starving, come on." She giggles as she pulls out of my hug and starts looking longingly at the restaurants on this floor of the shopping centre. "What are you in the mood for?" Elle questions me, linking our arms and dragging me towards the nearest eatery.

"I'm happy with whatever you fancy, Elle. My treat," I add, letting her know it's covered. I know they are fine for money, but I like to treat my sisters when I can.

"Hey, I was going to say that." She laughs as we enter the Greek restaurant closest to us. I guess she is starving, no looking around, just straight into the first place, and before I can say anything further, we are sitting down, and Elle orders us a meze and two glasses of wine.

"Aren't you driving?" I raise my eyebrow and smirk at her taking the piss. My sister is a lightweight of epic proportions.

"No, smart arse, I caught the bus in today." She sticks her tongue out at me, causing the waiter to smile at us as he writes down our order and heads off to get our drinks.

"So, little bro. What got your wig in a twist this morning?" Elle gets straight to the point, albeit gently.

The waiter arrives with our drinks, and I take that moment of reprieve to wonder whether I should even divulge the insecurities plaguing me. But Elle, being Elle, just thanks the waiter and then skewers me with a look that demands I spill everything. So I do, and she listens quietly, sipping her wine and nodding at me to continue when I falter or suggest I'm being paranoid until I have purged all the niggling feelings out and feel a sense of relief at their expulsion.

"Ben," Elle starts and seems to be grasping for the right

words. I take a sip of the tart liquid in my glass, barely tasting the fruity undertones as I await her verdict.

"We have all been through so much in the last few months. This year has been the worst I can ever remember, and that includes the year when I thought me and Jim were going to break up when I had depression after Beth was born. I can't stress how important it is for you two to communicate." She moves her glass to the side as the waiter places our food down on the table, and we hum our thanks without really registering his presence.

"You need to speak to Raz. Tell him how you feel. Where you see your relationship heading, and for goodness sake, tell him you want to move to Cornwall." Elle laughs at the last bit, shaking her head at the fact that I still haven't let Raz know I'm looking for a job down there or that I've had my eye on the housing market. She's right, of course. I need to speak to him about it.

"I know, okay. It's just never the right time, and he has only just started to come out of the haze that surrounded him the last couple of months. I don't want to bombard him with everything all at once." I know I'm making excuses, but I haven't felt that we had the right time to discuss anything serious.

Elle nods in understanding as she picks up a pork souvlaki skewer and starts to eat it.

"You know he loves you, right?" she says between mouthfuls. "It's obvious to anyone who sees the two of you together."

I know that he loved me, yes... but does he still?

Chapter SEVEN

RAZ

A small and non-descript text from Ben, informing me that he was having lunch with his sister, Elle, and wouldn't need much in the way of dinner tonight, had me replacing the ingredients I had pulled out of the refrigerator to make one of his favourite meals.

Jacket potato for one then. I guess he might want a small one, I muse as I search through our potato bag for one with fewer roots. Giving up, I dump the remaining tiny, shrivelled potatoes into the compost bin and decide it's time to get out of the house. I need some fresh air and a bit of shopping.

I'll get both whilst I'm out having coffee with Charlie.

The little café where we had lunch yesterday—*Was it only yesterday I met him?*—is slightly crowded, but I located Charlie with my second sweep over the interior. He is sitting right at the back. Charlie looks up at the same time as I spot him and waves, a large smile pulling across his face. I motion to him, asking if he wants coffee. I thought I'd grab us a cup before tackling my way through the tables and chairs.

Blowing on my fingers and cursing myself for forgetting my gloves, I begin to defrost. It's getting colder outside, and although it is fortunately bright and sunny today, it's freezing. As I order our coffee, I chance a look around at where Charlie is sitting, expecting him to be looking at his phone as half the customers in this place are doing, but instead, I find him looking at me with kind, searching eyes. I try not to read too much into it and return my attention to the server who is asking for my order. After requesting one large cappuccino and a latte, just the same as yesterday, I force down the little pang that has me wishing I was meeting Chloe for coffee so that we could set the world to rights just the way we used to. My heart grows heavy with the loss of my best friend, and I force a smile on my face and thank the barista for our coffees as I place my card over the machine, and it takes the payment.

I work my way through the crowded tables and chairs. The air is thick with the smell of coffee and cakes. The low rumble of conversation and the clatter of cups, plus the steamer on the large industrial coffee machines, add to the ambience of the place, giving it a cosy feel. Yet it does little to warm the cold sadness that has crept through me as I let my thoughts wander.

"You okay?" Charlie asks as soon as I place the mugs

down and move the chair out to take a seat.

"Yeah, you?" I lie as I shrug my coat off and place it over the back of my seat before sitting opposite him at the small table for two.

"Raz," Charlie reaches over and touches my hand. I pull back and wrap my fingers around my coffee mug, unable to meet what I know will be a kind but concerned gaze.

"We've only known each other a day, and already I know you're lying. If you don't want to talk about it, that's okay, but I'm a good listener," he says as he picks up his own mug blowing gently across the rim to cool the hot liquid. My gaze locks onto his lips for a minute before I meet his eyes. As expected, those deep chocolate pools are full of concern, but he's not pushing for answers. He sits patiently, waiting for me to talk to him.

The knot inside me tightens, and I blow out a breath to try and release it.

"I probably shouldn't have come." I let my thoughts out through my lips without checking them first, and he looks taken aback.

"Why? You aren't doing anything wrong, just meeting a new friend for coffee. I can see that you need to get something off your chest. Take your time." His kind words drift over me like a balm. He's right, I'm not doing anything wrong, but I do need to tell Ben about him. Just thinking that makes me feel a bit better. I'd already mentioned to Charlie that I was in a relationship when we spent the afternoon together yesterday. It's one of the things that we found we had in common.

Taking a sip of the milky liquid in my mug, I collect my thoughts in some semblance of order and begin to release some of the problems and feelings that have me tied up in knots today. Charlie listens as I purge, nodding and commenting in all the right places, just sitting there drinking his coffee.

"Let's get some lunch. Then we can swing by mine and pick up Duke," Charlie suggests as we finish our coffee. I remember that I need some shopping for tonight, so we do that and grab a sandwich from the local supermarket, deciding to eat in the park once we have Duke. Charlie's house is similar to ours but looks a little bit more lived in. Duke bounds to the door to meet us as soon as we arrive, and I take a moment to fuss over him before Charlie grabs his lead, and we head out again.

Duke trots beside us, occasionally nudging my hand with his nose. "He senses you aren't happy." Charlie acknowledges as we find a bench to sit on. I'm thankful that it's not raining, but I pull my coat up around my neck to fight off the cold wind.

"I'm not sure what happiness is anymore. I thought I was feeling better yesterday, but today I'm second-guessing everything, and right now, I miss Chloe so damn much." I've already told him about Chloe and a little about what happened without going into it too much. I've not even discussed in detail with Ben what we witnessed in that basement. The smells and sight of it still haunt my nightmares.

"Have you thought any more about counselling?" Charlie asks, pulling the plastic cover off the sandwich packet and removing a tuna and cheese sandwich from its confines. Duke sits dutifully between us, eyeing our lunches.

"Do I need counselling? It didn't happen to me." Even to me, my excuse sounds a little lame. Ben has been trying to get me to seek help since it happened, and I've refused. Because I'm fine, I just need to work through this myself.

"We've covered this already, Raz. It doesn't have to happen to you for you to be affected by it, and you clearly are," he says gently, and I know he means well, but the guy barely knows me, and it gets my back up a little. "Look, we barely know each other, but as I said to you yesterday, I can tell when people aren't quite themselves. Added to that, Duke was instantly protective of you. I'd say you need to talk to someone, but that's just my opinion," he adds as if he read my thoughts, which shakes me a little.

"You aren't as closed off as you think you are. It's there on your face for everyone to see." Charlie mentions when I ask him how he knew what I was thinking. I'm not sure that's true because I've been shutting myself away for months trying to deal with this shit by myself. Ben has had so much to deal with and has been grieving. I didn't want to add to his burden, and I said as much to Charlie as we finished our sandwiches and threw the rubbish in the nearby dustbin before walking around the park again with Duke.

"Don't you think that maybe the choice is Ben's? From what you've told me about him, I don't think he would feel that you are burdening him. More like sharing?" His words strike home as I take all that he has said in and think about the recent months, and the heated words whispered on my skin last night.

Our connection had been strong right from the very first moment when I noticed him looking at me across the crowded bar. Chloe had dragged me out dancing after another failed attempt at tracking down Damon. She wanted to let loose and feel free for a night, and I was always happy to be her partner in crime.

I had felt Ben's eyes on me before I even spotted him out with a group of work colleagues. He was dressed in suit trousers and a shirt, with his sleeves rolled up, and a bottle of beer in hand. He tipped his head towards the bar and gestured with the beer in his hand. He was looking at me like he wanted to devour me, and it sent a delicious shiver through me. I wondered how he could tell I was gay. I'd hidden that part of me for so long, and I was there dancing with my friend. Although Chloe was by then dirty dancing with some guy behind her. When she noticed me giving Ben the eye, she gave me the signal that everything was fine and shooed me away. My lips curl up as I remember the sparkle in her eyes and her desperate need for a debriefing the next day after sharing a taxi home with Ben, who made it perfectly clear that he was into me. Honestly, I've never been into public displays of affection, but the kiss he gave me before he got out of the taxi at his address, had me rethinking, for that night anyway.

A hand on my arm stops me from crossing the road in front of a car. I had been so lost in thoughts of Ben and of images of our time together that I had totally spaced out.

"Steady, Raz. I can see you have a lot to think about, so I'm going to head off. Will you be okay?" Charlie asks, looking at me again with sympathetic eyes. He really is a caring man. I can see why he is so good at his job and thank whatever fate brought us together yesterday because, with his help, I am finally seeing the light. Just as I did yesterday, I leave him feeling happier and lighter about my situation and in desperate need to talk to my boyfriend.

Pulling out my phone as I amble along towards our house, I find a message from Chloe and one from Ben saying we need to talk. Dread fills me immediately as my mind starts making up scenarios where Ben has had enough of me and wants us to split up. Where would I go? I don't belong anywhere anymore. My best friend is in Cornwall. Maybe I could go there?

My hand shakes as I reach inside my pocket and retrieve my key. A failed attempt later, and I'm finally inside, shutting the door and blasting the heating on as I'm freezing from spending so much time out in the cold. Plus, this message has sent a chill through me. I place the shopping bag on the kitchen counter, so caught up in my turmoil I don't register his presence straight away.

"Where were you? I leave work early to come and talk to you, and you're out. No reply, no nothing. What's going on, Raz?" Ben's words sound angry, but his voice is quiet, focused, and he doesn't even mention how he scared the life out of me creeping up behind me like that.

"I was out getting shopping." I turn around to face him.

"All afternoon?" Ben asks me, looking at me pointedly. "I sent that text after lunch, and you've only just looked at it." He sighs, looking resigned, and my heart almost stops. *Fuck, say something, Raz. Do something!*

"I met a friend. Well, I met him yesterday actually, but I haven't had a chance to tell you yet. We went out for coffee, then got lunch." My words peal out of me one after the other, sounding a lot like a confession.

"You've been out with another man?" Ben advances on me, his eyes questioning, roaming my face, my body. Is it wrong that I'm turned on by his obvious jealousy? *Focus, Raz!*

I need to stop this getting out of hand and keep ahold of that light feeling I had before I entered the house, before I saw Ben's text.

"His name is Charlie. I met him in the park yesterday. I needed to get out of the house and his dog, Duke, nearly knocked me over." I laugh slightly as I recall being accosted by the large Great Dane.

"So, how did you end up going for coffee with this Charlie two days in a row?" Ben's words sound even and enquiring, but I didn't miss the flash that went through his eyes when he said Charlie's name. Much as the sexual tension coming off Ben is giving me all the vibes, I don't want him to get the wrong impression. Giving him a brief rundown of what has transpired so far and reassuring him that we are just friends and that I needed someone to talk to seems like the best option. Only I might not have phrased it right because Ben is getting closer, not backing off, and as my back hits the kitchen counter, I wonder if I've actually made matters worse, not better.

"You could talk to me, Raz," Ben growls, grabbing the nape of my neck, pulling my head to his so our foreheads touch, and I go willingly, needing his touch and his jealous dominance more than I thought I would. Ben always seems to know what I need long before I have a clue, and it's one of the many reasons I know this man is it for me.

"I want to know everything that's going on in that brilliant mind of yours." His breath mingles with mine, and his words have me pushing forwards to close the gap between our lips. To an outsider, Ben is calm, gentle, a provider. He cares for all those he loves, deeply and completely. For me, he is all those things and more. The Ben I get to see when his eyes flash with pure dominant lust is the one I love the most.

Chapter EIGHT

BEN

When I used my flexi-time to come home early, I intended to have it out with Raz. To get everything I'd been storing inside my head out in the open, including these stupid ideas that he might be seeing someone else. But when I found him not home or answering the text I sent him, I started to spiral, scenarios creating themselves in my head one after the other. I've got so used to him staying in all the time since the blackness descended on him that I'd almost forgotten that he had a life outside these four walls.

Then he mentioned Charlie, and I'd say I saw red, but to be fair, it was likely green. I can't stand the thought of someone touching Raz or getting to see him the way only I do. Ordinarily he's no pushover, but his current mood has him down so far that he just agrees to anything right now, but when he's with me, fuck.

I bring my other hand up to hold his face to mine as he

kisses me like I'm all he will ever need, and I'm down with that. He is my forever, even if I haven't been able to tell him in so many words just yet or garner the promise that he will be mine until death parts us, which is why I won't allow this new friend to interfere in our relationship. I have no issue with Raz making new friends, but something in my gut is warning me that this Charlie is something different.

"I want to open up to you, Ben. I need to…" Raz's breathless voice has me hard as nails. Talking can wait.

"Oh, you'll open up for me, babe. You're going to open that tight arse for me and take me the way I know you can." I thrust my tongue in his mouth, swallowing his moans as his body jerks against mine, desperately seeking more. His cock is hard, rubbing up against mine in his jeans. The friction feels good, but it's not enough.

Taking my hand off his face and neck, I run them over his shoulders and down his sides until I reach his jeans. I pull my hips back just enough to reach his zipper and tug it down while trying to remember which drawer we stashed the small bottle of lube in. Back when we couldn't keep our hands off each other, I regularly fucked him over the table. Just thinking about that makes me groan impatiently as I reach inside his jeans and grip his cock in my hand.

"Take them off," I insist, turning away briefly as I remember which drawer it's in and opening it, grab the pump from underneath the tea towels we store there. I watch Raz's pupils dilate as he hurries to pull down his jeans and boxers. The shopping he brought home with him is discarded on the counter, just as my plans to have a heart to heart are going to wait because, right now, I need to be inside him, to own him in a way that I know he wants and I need.

I place the lube down on the kitchen counter as I start to unbutton my shirt, letting it drop down over my shoulders and onto the floor. Raz straightens up and walks over, running his hands over my chest and leaving goosebumps in the wake of his touch.

"I don't want to put a dampener on this. Whatever this is,"—Raz waves his hands around—"but you said you wanted to talk, and it sounded serious." His tone is hushed, and I can already tell he doesn't want to stop as I watch his eyes track down my body to the obvious bulge in my suit trousers. He sucks his bottom lip in between his teeth, as I slowly begin to undo the zipper.

"We'll talk later. Right now, I'm going to fuck you. Hard." I add the last part and relish the intake of his breath as my trousers pool at my feet. My erection bobbing and barely contained in my boxer briefs as I step out of them. "Raz…" his name comes out in a frustrated growl, needing to tell him my overwhelming desire to lay claim to him here and now. The thought of anyone with him has sent me into a frenzy. He looks me in the eyes and closes his briefly, letting out a long exhale of what sounds to me like relief as he grabs the pump from the side and moves over to the kitchen table. He puts the bottle down on the top and completely moves the chair out of the way. Pushing his hips back, he rests his palms on the table, looking over his shoulder at me.

Stepping out of the clothes now piled on the floor where I've pulled off my shoes to join them, I pad over on socked feet, not caring that we are both barely undressed. The sound of his short pants almost has me running over and thrusting into him. He's poised, vulnerable, something I know he hates except when it's for me. It's something that is only mine, and it will always be *only* mine.

"Keep your hands on the table." I manage to get the words out through gritted teeth. I'm so unbelievably turned on by the sight of him ready and waiting for me. His hips seem incapable of staying still as he twitches; his breathing becomes deeper. Running my hand down his back, I hold him still for a second, the electric energy between us making my cock leak. I grip it in my left hand, pumping slowly to ease the aching need.

"Ben…" I look up, my gaze having fixated on his tanned arse cheeks. He's watching me with hooded eyes. Reaching over, he picks up the pump and hands it to me, breathing heavily. He feels this just as much as I do, this pull we have always had towards each other. This connection which I was worried had somehow become severed. It's still here, humming between us with a life of its own. Taking the bottle, I squeeze a good amount and spread it over my cock, closing my eyes to the feeling of the cold lube against my burning skin. "Fuck." Were those his words or mine? I don't know because when I open my eyes, he's facing the table again. The grip of his hands on the top is whitening his knuckles.

I cover my fingers liberally, dropping the bottle to the floor beside us as I grip his hip with one hand, then run my lubed-up digits between his cheeks and over his puckered hole as he thrusts gently towards me. "Fuck. Yes, Ben," Raz half yells, half groans as my fingers breach the tight band of muscle. He starts to chant my name, spurring me on as I scissor and try hard to go slower. It's been a while, but I can't stop myself. My cock is weeping, begging me to take him. His voice grows hoarse as desperation takes over his tone. He wants to fist his cock so bad. I know this because, dammit, I want to do that too. I should take more time, but even as the thought enters my head, my body moves, and my cock joins my fingers. Raz whimpers as I remove my hand only to replace it with the pulsing head of my hard length, the one which is ruling my brain right now as it comes into contact with his slippery hole.

Pulling back his arse cheeks with both hands, I watch, mesmerised, as my cock disappears after the initial resistance. Raz sharply inhales a sound mixed with pleasure and pain, stilling my movements briefly as I allow him seconds to get used to the feeling of being filled and let him relax a little. That's all I can give him, seconds because without conscious thought, I'm moving again, pushing forward inch by fucking amazing inch. As I disappear inside him, I think I might explode like a pubescent teen.

"So fucking tight, babe. So fucking *mine*." I thrust forwards till he is impaled on my dick, making him yell out my name and more profanities as he takes all that I'm giving him. Again, I still as I let go of his arse, grab his hip with one hand, lean forward and find his cock with my other hand.

"Oh my God, Ben, fuck!" Raz all but screams as I grip him tightly in my hand and pump in time with my thrusts. Keeping it as slow as I can, savouring every moan and cry from his lips. We both know that this pace won't last, so I make the most of it, hitting his G spot with every thrust. His cock engorges in my hand. He's going to come before me, and I want him to. I want him wrung out in bliss when I hammer into this tight fucking hole that has me in a vice-like grip.

Pulling back almost all the way, I slam into him, giving him fair warning of what's to come, and that's when I feel the hot cum on my hand as his neck muscles strain, and he almost loses his grip on the table. I let go of his cock and take his slender hips in a punishing grip which I hope will leave bruises because this man, trying to regain his breath in front of me, is mine. That is the last conscious thought I have as I let the pleasure take over and drill into him, causing inhuman noises to escape his lips and the table to squeak as it moves with every hard thrust.

As my balls tighten and I get ready to pump my load into his shaking body, I know that I never want this to end. This feeling of belonging, not just Raz belonging to me, but me belonging to him, body and soul.

Don't ever fucking leave me. I don't know if I say the words out loud, but they spiral around my head as, with a final roar, I let go and fall forward over his body and encase it with my own as my cock pulses out my release inside the man I love.

We remain like that, just breathing and joined intimately for what seems likes hours but is likely just a minute or two. As I pull back, letting my softening cock slide from Raz, he groans.

"Did I hurt you, babe?" I'm suddenly very aware that it's been quite a while since we had sex like this, and I wasn't in any way gentle. Cursing myself internally, I grip Raz's arm and turn his limp body towards me, helping him stand.

"That was intense." Is the reply I get as he allows me to fold him in my embrace. I tighten my arms around him as a chuckle escapes me.

"You do that to me, Raz. Bring out the possessive beast inside me."

Raz laughs gently against my neck. His soft kiss pulls a moan from me, and even though I'm spent, I want more of this, not just the sex, the closeness that we have right now as his arms seem to find their strength again, and he holds me tighter.

"Let's shower," he suggests, his words whispered against my skin. I nod my agreement, unable to find my voice. How could I ever have doubted this man? Raz grabs my hand, leading me away from the chaos in the kitchen and up the stairs to our room. Inside our little ensuite, he turns the shower on as I take my socks off and throw them in the laundry basket. Entering the white-tiled bathroom, I step into the large walk-in shower. That, a toilet, and a small basin are all that we have in here, but it is sufficient for our purposes. Raz looks tired but happy as the warm water runs down his face and over his gloriously naked body.

"Come here," he says, looking at me in a way that has been missing for months. His eyes are alive again. I move forward and spin around as he manoeuvres me to where he apparently wants me, and I go freely. Hearing the sound of a bottle squeezing, I have a few seconds to guess what he is up to before his hands start roaming my body as he washes me. I let the sweet torture continue until he reaches my cock, then I spin around, taking him by surprise and pushing him up against the cold tiled wall of the shower.

"My turn." I laugh at the pout on his lips, sucking them into my mouth and causing him to moan as I deepen the kiss. I don't take it too far, though, because I want to wash him, and I know we can't hold this off much longer. We need to talk.

Chapter Nine

RAZ

Well, that escalated fast! I leave Ben in the shower, wincing a little. The ache brings a smile to my face as I bend over to pull on grey joggers. I don't often wear them, preferring jeans, but for comfort's sake and because I have no intention of leaving the house tonight, I relish the feel of the soft fabric as it glides up my legs. The shower stops, and I hasten to pull a T-shirt from my drawer. A humming growling sound is the only warning I get before Ben strides across the room and backs me against the wardrobe door.

"Not sure I'm going to be able to think straight with you in those. You know what they do to me." He smirks at me, his tone light and joking. My lips answer his, flooding me with a feeling of joy, one I have been missing for so long. I'm well aware of how he feels about joggers. Ben particularly loves how easy they are to pull down. I chuckle, lacing my arms around his neck and feeling his damp skin against my forearms. He is naked from the waist up, and I can't help but drink in his pale white skin. The tan he gained over the summer has faded now, but I still remember it well and the taste of sunshine on his skin.

Ben pulls back, but not before kissing me full on my mouth, lingering just that little bit too long as if reluctant to stop. I can almost physically feel the bricks of the bridge being built over the chasm that was expanding between us the last few months, and I don't want it to crumble.

"Why don't you get dressed and I'll go put the shopping away. I was going to put a couple of potatoes in the oven if you fancy one?" I ask, suddenly a little nervous about the discussion Ben wants to have. I watch as he turns to grab his own dark blue joggers, dropping his towel and pulling them on commando, making me groan as he bends over and throws me a huge grin over his shoulder. The man is trying to kill me, I swear.

"Yeah, I could go for a jacket spud. I seem to have worked up an appetite." He winks at me and then continues dressing. I can't help the smile that pulls at my lips, widening with every memory that floods my mind of the way he just owned me downstairs. That surely means he isn't tired of me and my dark mood? I feel light still, lighter maybe after what happened and how he washed me so tenderly in the shower, kissing me. He didn't mention love, but then he doesn't have to. It's not like I'm one to confess my undying love every five minutes either. It goes without saying that I do. I adore this man.

Not bothering with socks, I pad barefoot down to the kitchen and begin putting away the bits and pieces I purchased this afternoon. Was that just a couple of hours ago? It seems like a lifetime. Turning the dial on the oven so it heats up, I prepare the potatoes quickly and place them inside on a baking tray. Ben usually does most of the cooking because he enjoys it. Sometimes I would join him in the kitchen just to be near him and listen to his day, chopping the veg whilst he put the dinner together or just sitting at the kitchen table whilst we talked. The lightness slips slightly as I remember that it hasn't happened for months.

I put the kettle on to boil, deciding we might need something if we are going to sit down and talk. Reaching into the cupboard over the kettle, I grab two mugs and the teabags. The mundane task soothes me. Once made, I take the mugs of tea into the lounge expecting to find Ben there, but he's not. Placing the mugs down on the solid wood coffee table, I walk back through the doorway that leads to the hall.

"Ben?" I angle my head towards the stairs and shout up at him. A creak at the top of the stairs makes me look up. Ben stands there with a phone in his hand; when he looks at me, he isn't really seeing; his eyes are glazed over, and as he slumps to the floor, legs hanging over the stairs, I dash up them.

"What's the matter?" I ask, my eyes raking over him to see if he is hurt anywhere.

"They've deemed Jason and Carl's death accidental." Ben's face is even paler than usual. I know that they all thought that Marilyn was to blame for causing their deaths but seeing his face now, I guess he had pinned a lot of hope on them finding her guilty, of having someone to blame for the heartache and devastation caused to his family.

"We knew that it was likely they wouldn't find any evidence of foul play, Ben." I try to keep my voice as soothing as possible, but I know that it's not what he wants to hear.

"Carl never cooked. Why would he leave the gas stove on?" Ben asks the same question they have all been asking since it happened. "They were there at the dining room table; Jason was doing his homework. I expect Carl was helping him." This isn't something I don't know, but I'll let Ben get it out again.

"They wouldn't have known the gas was on, Ben," I reassure him of that. It's all I can do. None of us knows what happened in those final hours. All we know is that Marilyn had taken herself out for the night, but this wasn't unusual. She hated having Jason stay with them. That was apparent by the way she treated him, especially when Carl wasn't in hearing range. Jas had told his mum recently all that had been happening, he hadn't wanted to rock the boat or upset his dad, but it had been getting worse. Jen had booked an appointment to seek legal advice, although she didn't want to stop Jason from seeing his dad.

"He would have left Marilyn given more time. I'm sure

of it, and if he knew what had been going on he wouldn't have stayed there or had Jason over to stay. He loved Jen still and doted on Jason." I let him just purge his thoughts as they come to him. We all know Carl messed up and left Jen because he had cheated on her with Marilyn. It was a mistake, and he tried to do the right thing. The divorce had been amicable enough, but Jen had been devasted. Carl still spent a lot of time at the house with them, especially recently. Would they have reconciled? I don't know. Jen said they were managing to be friends, but she wasn't sure she could ever love him that way again after he betrayed her. All that makes no difference now. Nothing will bring them back.

"I need to see Jen." Ben snaps out of his daze and barely looks at me as he gets up and rushes down the stairs to the door. He toes on his shoes as I sit there at the top of the stairs just watching. *Does he even realise I'm here?*

"Do you want me to drive you?" I ask, thinking that it might not be a good idea for him to drive in this state.

"Fuck, sorry, Raz. No, it's okay, you haven't eaten, and I don't know how long I'll be. Matt's meeting me there because Elle can't get away right now. Jen's on her own." He looks at me, beseechingly asking me to understand that he needs space to be with his family, and I wish I could, but it hurts that he is pushing me away.

"Sure, no worries." I manage to push the words through lips that are faking a small smile, lying that it's okay.

"Raz?" He's finally looking, really focusing on me, and

I feel stupid for feeling this way.

"It's okay, Ben, you need to go. We can talk when you get back. Give Jen my love." I sing-song the last part as he pulls on a jacket and heads out the door with a nod, lost in thought again.

This is what I haven't seen. I've not been paying attention. So lost in my own darkness, I haven't paid attention to Ben's, and it hurts.

I walk down the stairs slowly, thinking of all the times I should have been with him when he went to his sister's. I guess he no longer considers bringing me as an option. I need to rectify that, to show him I can support him. Pulling my phone out of my pocket, I text the only other person I know understands me more than I understand myself—Chloe.

Then while I await her reply, I busy myself chucking Ben's mug of tea away, drinking mine and getting some fillings ready for the jacket potatoes. He's right, I am starving, and the slight ache I feel when I sit down to finally eat after making sure the kitchen and all of downstairs is clean and tidy brings a smile to my face as I remember the way Ben took me over this very table I am sitting at now. The thought lightens my mood, and as my phone dings, I get excited about chatting with Chloe. Only the message is from Ben.

Ben: Sorry, Raz, I'm going to be late home. Jen isn't in a good way, and I don't

want to leave her. Matt has gone to get shopping, and I'm going to cook something for them to eat.

What do I say to that? Anything other than it's okay would sound selfish right now.

Raz: Okay, I'll put your potato in the fridge when it's cooled.

I type it out, then delete the bit about the potato because that's pointless and will only make him feel bad. That's not what he needs right now.

Ben: I'm sorry.

Fuck, see, even the word okay wasn't right.

Raz: No need to be sorry, baby. Jen needs you.

Although it enters my head, I don't add 'more than I do' because it's not true. I need him too, but also, it just sounds needy. Fuck sake, when did I get so unsure. The old Raz was much more sure of himself, much more in control, *much more fun,* an unhelpful voice adds in my head. I physically shake myself and throw the rest of my dinner in the bin. I'm no longer hungry and really at a loss of what to do with my evening. Chloe hasn't replied, which isn't that unusual anymore but still smarts a little.

I shuffle from one foot to the other, unable to keep still. Desperate to take my mind off of all that's happened. We never had the discussion that Ben had left work early to have. Was it important? The edges of my mind are starting to darken, and I can't even go outside for a walk; it's pouring with rain and pitch-black now. The walls are closing in as my thoughts and emotions war with each other inside my head. It takes a second for me to realise that my mobile is buzzing in my pocket. Pulling it out, I answer without looking to see who it is. Anything would be a welcome distraction right now, even a telesales call.

"Raz? That you?" The voice is hard to distinguish against the background noise of what sounds like a pub or restaurant. "It's me, Charlie. I'm down at the local, and there is a live band I think you'd like. Why don't you come and join us?"

How could he have possibly known that I was on the edge again? The music I can hear in the background does sound good. Maybe this is the distraction I need. An hour or so wouldn't be too much, and as Ben isn't here anyway...

"Sure, which one are you at?" I ask, as there are several pubs in our area.

"Red Lion. Text me when you are nearly here, and I'll look out for you." His voice is loud against the silence of this house.

I shoot off a text to Ben, telling him I'm going out. Then put my phone on silent. A quick change from my joggers into a pair of tight-fitting jeans and a T-shirt, and I'm ready to go. Grabbing a jacket from the hooks by the front door, I ensure that I've left a light on and slip on my trainers—no need for anything posh as it's only a pub. I'm just about to leave when

I grab an umbrella as an afterthought and then head out into the cold rain. Hopefully, the walk there will clear my thoughts. A little company, a few pints of beer. That's bound to help.

Chapter TEN

BEN

I should have brought him with me, and I kick myself all the way there. Even Jen asks where Raz is, and she's grief-stricken at the verdict. Like me, I think she needed someone to blame for the horrific 'accident' that caused the death of her son and ex-husband. Matt is angry, and that's clear from the look on his face as he tries to hold in his emotions for Jen and let her be the one who is suffering. I recognise that because it's what I have been doing too, and not just with Jen.

Tonight, I intended to discuss it all with Raz, to lay my cards on the table, then I got distracted and ridiculously jealous. I rang Mum on the way over, asking her what we could do to help Jen. I know she doesn't want to move back in with my parents, but equally, she can't stay in this house, not just because she can't afford it but also because the memories are tearing her apart. Jen doesn't need to say this.

A BRIDGE TO FOREVER

We can all see it, but she confirmed it just now as we sat together on the sofa. I wrapped her up in my arms, and Matt pulled the blanket over her, then went to get some food. She finally exhausted herself from crying, and I gently lay her down on the sofa, tucked up in the blanket and went to the loo quickly, shooting off a short text to Raz.

I could tell by his response that he wasn't happy, and again I berated myself for not bringing him over. I'd just got so used to him not wanting to do anything or go anywhere that I guess I took it for granted that he wouldn't want to come even though he did offer to drive. I was just about to ring Matt and ask if he could possibly go round ours and get Raz when a text came through from Raz telling me he was going out. Out where? With who? Should I ask, or was that just the green-eyed monster again?

"Ben?" Jen's voice has me placing my phone down on the counter in the kitchen where I had wandered, intending to make the call to Matt. I hasten into the lounge to find Jen looking around frantically.

"It's okay. I'm here. I was just in the kitchen. Matt's gone to get some food. We noticed your fridge was empty earlier, so I'm going to cook you some dinner when he gets back." I move over to her and sit next to her on the sofa. Taking her hands in mine, I look at her, seeing the black smudges under her eyes, the unshed tears glassing them over. Her face is red and blotchy, with lines where she has been sleeping on the sofa. "Jen, you need to start taking better care of yourself." I try to keep my tone as sympathetic as I can, but the glare on her face suggests it wasn't.

"Take care of myself? For what? What have I got left, Ben? What is there to take care of myself for?" Jen starts to sob, and I pull her close, letting her tears soak my T-shirt once again. What can I say? Goodness knows I understand why she feels like that.

"You have us." Matt's voice startles both of us, and I jolt up from the sofa, preparing to fight anyone who wishes to harm my sister. He places the shopping down by the door, toes off his shoes, and walks over to Jen, giving me a nod. I squeeze Jen's shoulder and take the reprieve Matt is offering, letting him take my place to talk to her while I go and prepare us some food. Who knows when she last ate anything.

I let the rumble of their voices wash over me, feeling helpless once again. I text Mum telling her the situation, and she instantly texts back saying she will be over with Dad once they've finished dinner. Mum says she's going to suggest Jen goes away with them for a while, and I hate myself for feeling relieved. However, thinking about Jen going away sparks an idea in my head, and I pick up my phone, shooting off a quick text to Chloe. Maybe a break away is what Raz and I need too. A weekend out of this city could be just the right setting for that discussion I'm desperate to have with him.

Now that I feel a little more in control, I start putting away the shopping as Mr Whiskers, Jason's cat, winds himself around my legs. I leave out the ingredients for a quick pasta sauce, plus the red wine Matt obviously bought for Jen as it's her favourite merlot. I open the bottle leaving it to breathe for a moment while I busy myself feeding the cat, then chopping onions and veg to add to the tins of tomatoes I found in the cupboard. Matt also brought some bacon lardons, so I fry those off in a separate pan and grate some cheese before pouring a small glass of wine for me and large glasses for Matt and Jen. He's been staying here the last few nights, giving Elle and me a night off. None of us think it's a good idea for Jen to be alone in the house right now, so we have all taken it in turns, along with Mum and Dad, to stay here at night with her.

I turn off the hob before taking the glasses into the lounge. I'm even more careful about that now, and although Jen has carbon monoxide monitors, I'm not taking any chances. Carl was so careful here to make sure they had all the alarms along with the security they needed. I just don't understand why he didn't insist on monitors at Marilyn's place.

Matt half gets up and takes the glasses from me. "Thanks, Ben," he says, passing one to Jen. A look of concern crosses his face as she takes a hefty swing from the glass, nursing it in her lap as she swallows. Like me, Matt prefers beer, but both of my sisters are red wine fanatics, so we just go with the flow when drinking with them.

"I'm just putting the pasta on so dinner won't be long.

Also, Mum and Dad will be here soon." I glance at Matt, and a look of understanding flits through his eyes before he focuses them on Jen, who turns towards me.

"You didn't have to call them, Ben. I'm a big girl. I can take care of myself." She places the glass of wine down on the side table nearest her.

"I know, Jen, but you need to know that we are all here for you and as for taking care of yourself. I'm not sure that you are doing that right now." I hold up my hand to stem off the argument that looks about to fly from her lips.

"You're not, Jen, and I'm not saying that I don't understand, but let us help you. Okay?" I try to keep the forceful tone to a minimum. My sister has never been great at taking advice from me, stupidly believing that she knows better than me as she is older. Sometimes she does, but not now, not about this.

"Ben's right, Jen. You need to let us help you." Matt rubs her hands which are wringing the life out of the blanket that covers her knees. "Let's eat dinner together at the table, and then when your parents arrive, maybe we can come up with a plan? What do you say?"

We both wait with bated breath. I expect an explosion of some sort as my sister is not usually one to take things lying down. So, I'm somewhat surprised when she breathes out a shaky, "Okay."

"Okay," I repeat, nodding. "I'll go get us some food, then we can talk."

Dinner goes relatively smoothly, and we manage to persuade Jen to eat some, which is a plus. When Mum and Dad arrive, we all sit down in the lounge with tea this time, no alcohol, as I'm driving, and Matt and I quietly agreed that we all need a clear head for this intervention.

That's what this feels like. My sister is spiralling, and whilst that is to be expected, I don't want to lose another member of my family. My parents are pretty calm as they suggest that Jen spends some time away from the house with them in Cyprus. Mum has been looking at villas and hotels, and although she shows Jen some, my sister doesn't seem that enthusiastic and uses the excuse that the house needs sorting and she needs to take care of Mr Whiskers. After a lengthy discussion, we persuade her that Matt would sort the house with our help and take care of the cat and that a few weeks away might be just what she needs. Nothing is going to bring her son back, and she needs to grieve properly. Maybe being away from here and the stress that being around all of Jason's things and the memories this house brings will help her to heal a little, or at the very least bring her out of the self-destructive mindset she is in right now.

Jen eventually takes one of the sedatives the doctor gave her, and Mum puts her to bed.

"We'll stay here tonight. Give you both a rest," Dad says, shaking Matt's hand. "You have been such a support for her with all that you must be going through yourself. I'm very grateful."

My dad isn't usually one to show much emotion, but since Jason's death, he has been more vulnerable. They idolize their grandchildren, and to lose one is unthinkable. I pull Dad in for a quick hug, feeling his grief as acutely as my own. His body seems a little thinner, frailer than it ever did before. Dad pulls away and starts gathering the mugs to take to the kitchen, shooing us out when we try to help.

"You two go." He nods towards the door. Matt and I dutifully do as we are told and don shoes and coats, pulling the door shut behind us. I breathe in the night air as we exit, thankful that the rain has stopped, and all that is left is the damp smell hanging in the crisp cold breeze.

"You doing okay?" I ask Matt, who hasn't moved towards his car yet. "Need a lift home?" I offer, which seems to bring him out of whatever thoughts he was trapped in.

"Yeah, do you mind? I'm shattered, and honestly, although I didn't drink much of that wine, I think it's better if I don't drive. I'm just feeling drained, you know?" He looks over at me, and I can see how tired he is. His broad shoulders are stooped a little, and the dark circles under his eyes tell me he hasn't slept any better than the rest of us.

"Sure, come on. I'll drop you on my way home." I gesture towards my car, and he starts walking towards it as I press the unlock button on my keyfob. Once we are on our way and heading towards Matt's house, I feel the silence pressing in. I've known Matt for quite a few years, but I'm rarely alone with him, and it feels a little awkward somehow.

"I think I'm going to decorate and tidy the house up while Jen's away. Get it ready for selling." Matt's voice sounds loud in the quiet interior of the car, and I don't miss the hint of pain there.

"It's for the best, Matt, and she can't afford to keep it." I try to reassure him that cutting the last tie to his brother and nephew, or son as it turns out—still can't get my head around that—is for the best.

"Yeah, I know. I just can't believe he left her in such a mess. I'm so sorry, Ben. What must you think of my brother? He was a good person, I promise. He just made mistakes." Matt runs his hand through his short hair and down his face;, the tattoos on his hand and arm illuminated in the street lights as I glance his way.

"Carl was an idiot, yes, but I'm not angry at him, Matt. I'm not sure Jen ever was either. She was just disappointed. He had everything and then threw it away for what? He wasn't happy with that bitch Marilyn, that was clear." I sigh, knowing we've had this conversation before but still feeling the need to reassure him that I don't hold his dead brother any ill will.

"I think he thought he was doing what was right, but he just got it so damn wrong." Matt sounds angry, and not for the first time, I wonder if he might harbour some feelings for my sister. I push that thought from my mind. It's late, and tonight has been a lot. My mind is being ridiculous. We make it to Matt's street without saying anything else. Both of us are lost in our own thoughts. As he gets out of the car, I suggest that I could help with the decorating, offering up my and Raz's services which he says he appreciates. Then he shuts the door, and I check that he gets in as I always do with friends before driving off.

I don't know what I expected to find when I got home, but it certainly wasn't another man helping Raz into our house. The lights show their silhouettes as the other man drags Raz closer to him. I park the car, feeling anger overriding the exhaustion I previously felt, as I get out in a hurry and lock it on the fob approaching them on heavy feet.

"What the hell are you doing?" I ask, trying not to shout as it's almost midnight, and I don't want to bring our nosy neighbours to the windows.

"You must be Ben," the tall, good-looking man says as he tries to straighten a giggling Raz up against the door frame. "I'm sorry I didn't realise he was such a lightweight." The man laughs, holding Raz as he sways and stumbles, preventing him from falling through the door by the amused looking guy next to him.

"I'm his boyfriend, yes." I feel petty pointing that out, but I don't give a shit right now.

"Hi, I'm Charlie. Sorry, we've had a few too many to drink at the local." The man extends a hand whilst holding Raz upright with the other. Reluctantly I shake it as I was always taught to be polite. "I wasn't sure that he would make it back here in one piece, so I thought I'd better walk him home," he adds as he lets go of my hand.

Charlie's voice betrays his drunken state with the slur on his words, although he appears to be trying to keep it together. Is that for my benefit or Raz's? I don't know, and right now, I don't care because I'm likely to say something I shouldn't in a minute.

"Well, thanks for seeing him back. I'll take it from here." My tone is abrupt, and Charlie ducks his head in acknowledgement as he pats Raz on the shoulder.

"Take care, Raz," he says as I reach out past him and hold Raz in place. Charlie steps back from the doorway, and as he passes, he looks me in the eyes and says, "Raz is hurting. He needed to let loose a little." Then he turns and leaves as I stare at his back. Does he think I'm angry that Raz went out?

Chapter ELEVEN

RAZ

My head is thumping, and my mouth feels like something crawled in there and died. *Fuck, what the hell did I do?* Images surface as my brain tries to assess the damage. I was at the pub with Charlie and some of his friends. The band was pretty decent. The beer was flowing, just the thought of that pulls a groan from my lips, and my stomach turns over. *Shit, how much did I drink?*

"Good, you're awake. I've left some painkillers by the bed and water. I suggest you drink that before you try moving. I have to go to work." Ben's voice sounds loud and not in the least bit happy. I crack open one of my eyelids, trying to adjust to the dim light leaking from the bathroom. Ben is pulling on his suit jacket over by the bedroom door. The hallway light is on behind him, so I can't see the expression on his face as it's shrouded in shadows, but I can feel his eyes boring into me like tiny bullets of disapproval piercing my skin. *Christ, what did I do last night? Did I say something I shouldn't?* My foggy hungover brain scrabbles to sort through images and snippets of conversation, coming up blank.

"Ben... I..." I should apologise. I'm not sure what for, but it feels like I should.

"Don't, Raz, okay. I haven't got time to get into it this morning, but I didn't need to be told by some stranger that you were hurting. If you are feeling that way, I need you to talk to *me*." He punctuates that last word, and my head starts to thrum with all the unsaid words.

"I know, Ben, I know, but talking and communicating isn't a one-way street." Now I sound angry, or maybe I'm just damn tired, and I don't mean to sound accusatory, but it came out that way because I have the hangover from hell.

"I've got to go." Ben turns and walks out the door without even a goodbye. Fuck.

I try to pull myself upright, but my body hates me for it, and I end up holding my head in my hands, sitting on the edge of the bed as the front door shuts downstairs. The chasm that I thought was beginning to be bridged has just opened up to Grand Canyon proportions. How the bloody hell did we get back here again? My stomach rolls, and I only just make it to the bathroom before I revisit my mistakes from last night.

After my body dispenses with my overindulgence, I shower and pull on my favourite jeans and T-shirt, trying to establish some form of normalcy in my life. There will be no workout session for me today. Once I feel more like myself, I take the tablets and down the water, then pick up my phone from the charging dock. I know I didn't put that there last night, so it must have been Ben. Guilt crushes me for a second, but I push it away. No sense in dwelling there, or it will suck me in, and I can't afford to spiral today. As I wander downstairs slowly, I check the messages on my phone, purposefully leaving the ones from Charlie for now.

`Chloe: Hey, arsehole, what are you doing out without me? Joking, it's great to see some new photos on Insta of you enjoying yourself. Did Ben take them?`

What pictures, oh fuck!

I bring up my Instagram app in a hurry. There in plain sight, for everyone to see, is a picture of Charlie and me with our faces smooshed together side by side, both looking a little worse for wear but with pint glasses in hand and smiles on our faces. I don't remember that being taken, but I clearly posted it, and Charlie, Aiden and several other friends of theirs that were out last night have been tagged. Well, that might explain Ben's mood, or it could be the incoherent me that he had to no doubt deal with last night after being at his sister's. Dammit, I didn't even think about what that was like last night.

`Raz: I got very drunk, Chlo. Ben wasn't with me, and I think I might have pissed him`

off.

My phone rings, and I sit down on the sofa to answer it, having not made it as far as the kitchen yet.

"What do you mean you pissed him off? Who was the man in the photo? What the hell is going on?" Chloe's voice rises with each word, and I have to pull the phone away from my head.

I set about trying to explain to her what's been going on. It's time I came straight with someone, and Chloe has always been my confidant and my cheerleader. She listens and hums in the right places, never judging or suggesting that I should have done things differently.

"Oh, Raz. Why didn't you tell me it had gotten so bad?" she asks finally and then adds, "I know I've been wrapped up in my own healing, but I've always got time for you. You're my best friend, and I miss you so much."

Her confession spears me with pain, and I have to admit how much I miss her, too. "Nothing feels right anymore." I hate sounding so weak, but I know Chloe is the only person who will understand.

"Look, I think you should both come down here for a long weekend. You need to sort this out, and Ben has already texted asking about places to stay." Chloe returns to her no-nonsense self, pulling a smile to my lips. It's so good to hear her returning to normal, to my Chloe.

"Chlo, I think you are right, but I'd have to check with Ben. Things aren't great with Jen right now."

Chloe murmurs her understanding but ends the conversation by suggesting that if Ben can't make it down, then I need to. "It's not up for discussion, my friend. I need you down here, and you need to figure out what you want in life. If needs be, bring your laptop. You can work down here, so don't use that as an excuse." She finishes all bossy and demanding, making me laugh out loud.

"I'll speak with Ben later and let you know. Can you ask Jay if one of the cottages is free, please?" Making a few rudimentary plans in my head. Time to grab some food and send an apology text to my boyfriend. We say our goodbyes, and I reassure her I am fine again before she will let me get off the phone. By the time I walk into the kitchen, I feel lighter than I did when I came downstairs. My stomach growls, letting me know it disapproves of our antics and that it needs some serious carbs to make up for it. Fishing around in our freezer, I come up with some sausages and hashbrowns. *Time for a little cooked breakfast, methinks.*

I put the oven on, then root around in the cupboard for a tin of baked beans. Grab some bread, eggs, and the toaster out of the other cabinet, and I'm all set. Part of me wishes Ben were here so I could make him some too. With that thought flitting through my mind, I grab my phone from the kitchen counter where I left it to make my freezer raid. Charlie's messages are still there, so after I place the tray with the sausages and hashbrowns in the oven, I open them up. A couple ask how I'm doing. One of them mentions Ben and asks if things are okay with us, but the one that draws my attention is the one asking if I would like to meet up tomorrow for lunch to discuss what happened last night.

What does that mean? I honestly don't remember much, and I can't possibly have done anything I shouldn't have. I wouldn't do that to Ben... I love him. Plus, I was never alone with Charlie. Then I remember walking home with him, but I was so drunk he held me up most of the way. I didn't do anything. I didn't!

Suddenly I don't feel all that hungry.

I will need to clarify with Charlie what he means because this could be a total disaster and wreck more lives than just mine and Ben's.

Placing my phone back down, I move around the kitchen on autopilot, putting away the eggs and toaster. I'll just eat the sausages and hash browns. I need something inside me. Coffee, that's what I need. I pick up the kettle, fill it halfway, and then put it on to boil. Reaching up, I pull a mug out of the cupboard, place it on the side, and begin to make coffee when there is a knock at the door.

I move as fast as my body will allow towards the door, hoping that it isn't Charlie—for some reason, I just don't want to see him right now. I breathe an almost audible sigh of relief as I open the door to find Matt standing there.

"Hey, Raz, I know it's early, but I just went to pick my car up from Jen's and thought I'd drop round. Ben said you'd be around today when he gave me a lift home last night."

Matt stands there, all tattooed six-foot solid muscle of him, and it takes me a second to react as he is the last person I was expecting to turn up at our door this morning. "I can come back?" He looks a little lost, and I immediately kick myself for not reacting quicker.

"Sorry, no, come in." I move to the side to allow him through the door. "I'm just a bit slow. Slightly hungover this morning," I add, trying to excuse my odd behaviour as I had just stood there staring at him.

"Rough night all round then," Matt states as he stands in the hallway. Well, that confirms that last night was no bed of roses at Jen's, and again I have to squash the immediate guilt that arises and threatens to consume me.

"I didn't see much of Ben this morning. He didn't mention you were coming round, sorry." I gesture towards the kitchen. "Do you want a coffee? I was just making myself some breakfast," I add as I follow him down the hallway with its walls of sage green sporting photos of me and Ben, looking happy and carefree, to the back of the house and into the kitchen. Matt looks around as he walks; I'm not sure he has ever been to our home before. I try to wrack my brain, but it's coming up empty as the fog hasn't entirely lifted yet.

"No, that's all on me. I thought I'd drop by and see if you could come and help me get some paint today. If you've got time," he adds the last part in a rush. I know it's an assumption made by many that if you work from home, you have all the time in the world to do anything you please. As it is, I don't have a lot to do today, so I confirm that I'm free whilst offering him some food, which he declines, saying he'd had some toast before leaving and would grab something later.

"Have a seat, Matt." I nod towards the kitchen table as I pour us both a coffee.

"Thanks. Look, I don't mean to intrude on your day. It's just I need to do something, anything to keep myself busy right now." His tone is strained as he sits at the table and takes the mug from my outstretched hand. I return to the table a moment later with my plate of food. Matt looks at it but makes no comment on my meagre meal, preferring to wrap his hands around his mug. He looks tired, and I'm reminded again that he must be dealing with a lot of grief.

"I'm sorry, Matt. For all that's happened. Are you doing okay?" I look at him as I absentmindedly start cutting my food.

"I'm just trying to be there for Jen. She's not doing well right now." He sighs, taking a sip of the dark liquid in his mug.

"That's not what I asked, Matt. Are *you* doing okay?" I emphasise the you, just as Charlie has to me several times, gently encouraging me to speak about my feelings rather than deflecting with other people's. I can see that Matt is struggling, and I wonder who he has to turn to. We aren't that close, but maybe that's a good thing. Sometimes it's easier to talk to someone you don't know that well. Or so I'm discovering.

"To be honest, Raz, I don't know. I think I'm still numb." He shakes his head as if to rid himself of whatever he was thinking, "I didn't mean to come here and burden you with my problems. How is Chloe doing?" Matt asks, putting down his mug, and I don't call him out on the subject change.

As I finish what I can of my meal, we discuss what happened, but like Matt, I can't go into detail or revisit my feelings from the day we found my best friend in the basement of a broken-down building. Instead, he fills the awkward silence with stories of Cornwall and Pendlebrook. I had forgotten that he hails from there himself, so it's a welcome distraction. By the time I've loaded the plate and our mugs into the dishwasher, I've agreed to come and help him choose paint and other decorating necessities from our local hardware supermarket. Apparently, he needed my flair for design or something equally suspect, but as I did choose the colour scheme for our house, I happily agree to it— anything to take my mind off my own problems.

Chapter TWELVE

BEN

My mood hasn't improved by the time I've gotten to the office. I don't even know why I'm so annoyed by it all. It's just a photo, Raz looked like he had a good time which should make me happy, but it doesn't. Which then makes me feel like a dickhead. My mood is further reduced by my boss telling me my team is needed in our London office this weekend. He reminds me that we aren't often called upon to work weekends, but it is part of our contract. So maybe my face gave away my lack of joy at this little snippet of news.

I don't look forward to breaking it to my team; they all have families and commitments over the weekend, so it won't go down well. We've all been lulled into a false sense of security because our boss wasn't wrong when he said we aren't called upon to work weekends often. I think I can count on one hand how many times I've stayed late on a Friday night or worked Saturday, and I've been here three years.

I inform Stu in the kitchen as I make hot drinks for everyone to soften the blow. He is as impressed as me, and the rest of the team takes it the same way. I put on a brave face, trying to make it sound appealing. We are being paid for travel and accommodation. I'm pretty sure they see right through me, though. As I check my phone around lunchtime, I bristle a little at the lack of communication from my boyfriend. Just as I'm about to text him, a message comes through.

Raz: I'm helping Matt get some paint for Jen's house. Likely be out all afternoon. I'm so sorry about last night. If I did or said anything that made you angry, just know that I didn't mean it. I'll make it up to you. Promise.

He signs off with a load of heart emojis and a sad face, making my lips curl up involuntarily. He's such a sap sometimes, and he was always the joker, always happy. Often that would be masking something else, but we never before had problems with communication. I could always tell when he wasn't feeling himself. But since Chloe was kidnapped and tortured, things have been different, and I know that it's not just with him. I've not been myself either.

Ben: We still need to talk, Raz. Things can't stay like this between us, and I'm not saying that it will be easy, but we both need to move forward, and I want to do that with you.

Three dots appear instantly, then stop. I wait for a moment, hoping to get a response, but there is nothing. As he's out with Matt, I'm going to assume that something has taken him away from his phone, and it's not that he doesn't want to reply to that. I just leaked a little of my heart out, not as much as I wanted to, but I guess I was hoping for some confirmation that we are both on the same page.

Moving along in the queue at our local sandwich shop, I push the phone back into my pocket and try to concentrate on the conversation going on around me between several of my work colleagues. We've all come here to get lunch and then brainstorm the project we are working on this weekend—a working lunch. Nothing unusual, but still, I crave something more. Something less all-consuming. A job where I can just do the work and then go home and spend my time with Raz. Is that just a pipe dream? Maybe we could get that dog we've talked about since we moved in together and take walks across the cliff paths? I'm so lost in my daydream; I don't realise that I've come to the front of the queue and the server is waiting to take my order. A sharp nudge to my ribs from Stu pulls my focus in front of me, and I rattle off my order of tuna melt, needing something warm as it's freezing outside. Not that it feels like that in here, the warmth inside this little shop is a little too much for my thick coat, which I pulled over my suit jacket before I came out of the office. Even now, the telltale trickle down my back tells me that my shirt is likely to be wet, and I'll have to keep my suit jacket on in the office when I get back.

The day drags on, and still no word from Raz, but I can't complain; he's helping Matt sort out my sister's house for selling. I got a text from Mum saying they are leaving this weekend; in her opinion, it was needed sooner rather than later, and I can't say I disagree. By the time I'm ready to leave, I've had enough. I'm tired, a little stressed, and the muscles in my shoulders are tense and bunched where I've been working at the computer all day. Driving home in the late-night traffic doesn't ease the tension, and by the time I get home, all I want to do is take a long hot shower and wash away the day.

"Raz?" I shout out his name as I walk through the door, hoping to find him home. A night in with my man is also much needed.

"In the kitchen." His voice sounds strained, and I'm immediately on high alert.

"You okay?" I ask as I hurriedly kick off my shoes and hang my coat up in the hallway. I leave my suit jacket on the bannister and roll up my sleeves, preparing to do battle with whatever has upset my boyfriend.

I stop at the doorway to the kitchen and take stock of what I am seeing. There are bowls and utensils strewn across every available surface. Condensation on the kitchen window and pans bubbling away on the stove. In amongst all this chaos stands a rather harassed looking man in joggers and an apron. My lips curl up at both sides, pulling at my cheeks as I let out a laugh I didn't know was coming, taking Raz by surprise as he looks up and blows out a breath of frustration.

"I wanted to have all this cleared up before you came home, but time got away from me." He glances around at the mess and looks a little sheepish as his eyes meet mine. The smile hasn't left my face as I take in his efforts and obvious discomfort.

"What are we having?" I ask, stalking slowly towards him, hoping my intent to kiss him thoroughly shows in my eyes because that's precisely what I intend on doing. Our eyes stay locked in an embrace of their own, and I'm surprised I don't bump into anything as my sole purpose is to get to this man.

The one you've been annoyed with all day? a stupid voice in my head asks, and I tell it to fuck off. God knows I haven't been a barrel of laughs to be around recently either. I have no right to get annoyed with him for finally trying to get out of the house and enjoy himself.

"I made a tikka masala from scratch." His voice is breathy as my fingers touch the stubble on his face. The rough feel of it against my skin makes my heartbeat increase. Need bleeds into every pore, pushing aside my tiredness.

"A curry, you say? From scratch?"

He nods, leaning into my palm, which has found its way

to his jaw, as I rub circles across his cheekbone with my thumb.

"You feeling very sorry?" I keep my voice light to show I'm joking. He really has nothing to be sorry for.

"So sorry," he whispers into my palm, kissing the inside before stepping closer and kissing my lips. The contrast of his soft lips and scratchy stubble against my face brings all sorts of thoughts to mind, but as his tongue swipes over my lips, demanding that I open, the hiss of water hitting the hob calls a halt to our kiss. Raz steps back, swearing softly under his breath and turns to deal with the pan that is boiling over, giving me an amazing view of his bare back—tanned skin and taut muscles that flex as he moves around the kitchen make me want to strip him out of those joggers, drop to my knees and take his tight arse right here in the kitchen. I want to pull those cheeks apart and—

"See something you like?" His tone suggests that he is making a joke, but there is something else in the background. Before I can put my finger on it, he flashes me a smile over his shoulder. "Dinner is ready. Did you want to change first?"

I shake my head, trying to rid myself of my lustful thoughts, but I make no attempt to hide how hard just looking at him has made me.

"No, it's fine, we can eat now. After all the trouble you have gone to, I think we should get this masterpiece served." I feel light, at ease, just as it always used to be between us.

However, most of the time, it was me doing the cooking, so for Raz to have gone to such trouble to make up for something he has no need to feel sorry for is a big deal, and I want to be sure he knows how much I appreciate it.

We spend the meal mainly chatting about my sister and her house. Raz spent a great deal of time with Matt today and agrees with me that he is not processing his grief properly as he is trying to take care of my sister. We near the end of our meal, which was delicious even if the rice was slightly overcooked and the naan was a little overdone. I say nothing about that, though; why would I? My boyfriend had just spent all day taking care of my family and then the rest of his time making a wonderful meal for us to enjoy together. At the back of my mind, I am very aware that our conversations over dinner have remained safely on subjects that don't involve our relationship, with not even a mention of the infamous Charlie or their night out, but I've enjoyed our easy chat too much to change the subject onto more serious matters. I'm happy and so much more relaxed than I was when I left work. Shit, that's one thing we need to discuss.

"I'll clear up while you go get showered, then we can watch that movie you've wanted to watch." Raz starts to get up from the table and grab the plates. The sight of his naked torso captures my attention.

"How about we both clear away and then head up to the shower?" I raise my eyebrow and then waggle them at him, enjoying the lighter, joking atmosphere between us.

"But I've already showered," Raz deadpans, and if I didn't see the telltale twitch of his lips, I'd think he was seriously turning me down.

A laugh pulls its way out of me as he finally cracks and chuckles as he takes our plates over to the sink. It's pitch-black outside, and I pull down the kitchen blind sealing us into our own bubble as we stack the dishwasher and wash and dry the pans. Amicably chatting about nothing significant, just enjoying each other's company. I take every opportunity to touch his naked skin relishing in his reaction to me. It's been like this since the very beginning with us, and with renewed determination, I intend to make sure it stays like that. With that in mind, as soon as we have finished clearing the kitchen, I drag my laughing boyfriend upstairs to the shower.

After what seems like hours in the shower, showing Raz just how much I love him and losing myself in his loving touch, we emerge stronger in our connection. As we lie snuggled up in bed, I feel so relaxed and at home finally. I can't help but wonder why I let my insecurities get the better of me.

"I love you so much, Ben." Raz turns his head slightly from his position on my chest, tilting his face up towards mine. "You know that, right?" he asks, his tone uncertain and eyes full of questions.

"Yes, I know, babe. Not as much as I love you, though." I joke, our standard response to each other when we are alone. Although I realise with a tinge of sadness that it has been a while since we said this to each other.

"More," he finishes with a grin, and my lips pull up in answer.

"Jay has a cottage free this weekend, so I thought we could go down to Pendlebrook and spend some quality time by the sea. Away from here. What do you say?" he asks. His face is lit up, and that question is so eager I hate myself for what I'm about to say.

"I can't, babe. I've got to go to London with work."

Even though he tries to hide it, Raz's face is too easy to read right now. The sad look that flits through his eyes before he blinks it away breaks my heart a little.

Chapter THIRTEEN

RAZ

Just like that, my perfect evening and, by extension, perfect weekend is ruined. I know it's not his fault, so I try not to show my disappointment, but I'm not sure I'm that good an actor. I had it in my head that we would take walks along the coastal paths, spend time in the pub with our friends and have lazy mornings in bed just the two of us for the whole weekend. Phones off and away from it all.

But I guess it's not to be.

"I'm sorry." Ben's voice breaks into my self-pitying daydream of all the things I wanted to do this weekend. "You should go still." He pulls my face upwards, and I have to move a little so that I can look at him properly.

"Not quite the same thing, baby." I wallow in my annoyance at the injustice of it all. He hasn't had to work a weekend for so long I'd forgotten that it was part of his job.

"I know, and we'll go again, together. But, I think it

would do you good. Get away from here, and you'll get to spend some time with Chlo."

"I'll ring her tomorrow," I concede, the idea of going to Cornwall suddenly really appeals, rather than spending the whole weekend by myself here. I have no doubt I could go out with Charlie and Aiden again, but to be honest, as much as I enjoy their company, I am missing my best friend something fierce and still don't feel myself yet. Maybe once I'm around her, I will.

We settle back down tangled up in each other under the duvet with the action film Ben has been dying to watch for a few weeks, and at some point, my eyelids start a steady descent, and I can't keep them open. I'm briefly aware of Ben turning off the telly and lamp by the bed before sleep claims me completely.

After a slightly fitful sleep, I wake up feeling like I could sleep several hours longer, but I'm determined not to let that creep in again. Many days have been wasted dozing in bed until lunchtime when the darkness refused to let me get up, and the nights were so sleepless that I felt incapable of moving in the mornings. Last night I woke up twice, once because I had a nightmare and the second time because Ben was talking in his sleep. He rarely does that unless he is stressed, and it never makes any sense. It's more noise than actual words, but he did say 'don't leave' at one point.

I slide my legs over the bed, giving my body time to adjust to this more upright position and listen for signs of

Ben in the house, having realised as soon as I woke up that he wasn't next to me anymore. A tiny clattering from downstairs suggests that he is in the kitchen. I stretch my toes and calves and then stand up, reaching above my head to work my muscles awake. I slept in my boxer briefs last night, so I grab my abandoned joggers, T-shirt and hoodie and pull those on before wandering downstairs to find Ben.

"Someone's up early," Ben greets me as I walk down the hallway and into the kitchen. He pulls a mug out of the cupboard as I move in behind him and wrap my arms around his waist. Ben's already dressed in a shirt and trousers and smells delicious. My hands span his chest feeling the exhale he makes as I bring my body closer and kiss his neck.

"Good morning." I smirk against his skin loving the moan my touch has drawn from him. Ben places the mug down gently on the sideboard and turns in my arms. Then, leaning against the countertop, he pulls me in close again so I can feel how hard he is for me.

"Every damn time, Raz." His forehead rests on mine, and I get lost in his gorgeous blue eyes.

I know what he means; even though we've had our difficulties with intimacy over the last few months, when things are more settled, his ability to turn me on is the same. Just one touch or kiss can ignite the passion we have always had for one another. Ben's breathing is heavy, but he pulls away from me a little. "I've got to go into work early. I was going to bring you a cup of tea before I left."

"Well, I can't let you go to work all frustrated now, can I?" My lips pull up in a broad grin as I take in his shocked expression.

"Babe, I've got to leave!" His tone is lust-filled and agonised over the need to leave and stay.

"I'd best make it quick then." I laugh at the indecision on his face as I reach between us, give his hard cock a squeeze then unzip his trousers.

"Jesus, Raz," Ben moans and widens his stance. He grips my shoulders, pushing me down on my knees; all the while, I can see that his mind is still trying to decide whether this is a good idea. I guess I'll help him with that. I free his cock from the slit in his boxer briefs, and without messing about, I grip the base and take him in my mouth; working my throat to accommodate his length, I start to suck, flattening my tongue against the underside. Ben moves one hand to the back of my head, clearly giving up any idea of stopping me as he starts to thrust forward.

I know just how much he likes to take control, and I relish in the freedom it gives me as I let him take over and hold tight to his thighs whilst he fucks my mouth with abandon. Breathing through my nose, I take him deep, challenging myself to take him deeper with each thrust. Ben pants above me with a chant of "Oh fuck," and "Yes, babe." If I could look up from this angle and see his face, I know he would be watching, getting off on the sight of me on my knees just as I do when the roles are reversed. His pace changes as he gets closer, and I let go of one thigh, moving my hand until I grasp his balls still inside his trousers and begin to massage them in my palm.

"Holy fuck!" he roars as hot cum spurts down my throat, and I hastily swallow, trying to catch every drop.

Ben slumps back against the kitchen counter, and I make sure to lick every inch of him clean before gently returning his cock to his boxers and zipping up his trousers. Then, getting to my feet, I give him a light kiss on the lips and move over to the kettle to make my tea with a huge smirk on my face. Within seconds he is behind me, crowding me against the counter and kissing my neck.

"If I didn't have to go right now, I would take that fucking tight arse over this counter. Fuck, Raz, that was one hell of a send-off. I don't want to leave you, babe, but I really do have to go."

His voice is husky with emotion whispering his words near my ear before he bites the lobe causing a moan to release from my lips. I'd forgotten what day it was, dammit. Ben leaves for London today.

"I didn't hear you pack." I try to keep my voice even. I'm not worried; I'm not.

"I was quiet. I didn't want to wake you. Raz, don't look so worried; it's only two nights tops. Anyway, you'll be in Cornwall."

"I haven't spoken to Chlo yet, but I'm sure it will be fine. I'll ring her in a bit and arrange it."

A BRIDGE TO FOREVER

"Look at me," Ben demands, turning me around with his hands. "It's going to be fine. I'm going to be fine." His eyes search mine. It's as if he can sense just how apprehensive I am about us being separated like this. I know it's stupid because he stayed at Jen's enough times over the last month. However, this feels different, and I can't help but worry about the unspoken conversation we have yet to have. The discussion he was so adamant we needed, but as of yet, there has been no 'right' time. Now there are things I want to say, to ask about our future. Things I didn't even realise I wanted until recently.

"You are overthinking this, babe. I'm just going to work. Then I'll be back." He puts on his best Arnie voice for the last bit, trying to lighten the mood, and I can't help but chuckle. Sometimes he's such a fool. I love that about him, though. Recently things have been way too serious around here, and it's time to bring back some of the fun we used to have. I take a deep breath steadying my nerves and lean over, wrapping my arms around his neck.

"You're right. It just feels wrong, but then a lot of things do. I'll go down to Pendlebrook and spend some time with Chlo and all the others. When we both get back, how about we go out for dinner?" I suggest wanting to get things back to normal and hoping that whilst we have dinner out somewhere with no distractions, perhaps we can talk about our future a bit.

"Yes, I'd like that." Ben kisses me lightly on the lips,

then moves away, grabs his suit jacket off the back of the chair by the kitchen table and then turns once more to look at me. "I'll text you when I get there, but I know you'll see I'm there before that." He smiles and then walks across the lounge and out into the hallway, where his overnight bag rests by the door. I didn't even notice it there in my haste to get down here this morning.

Ben waves before letting himself out of the door, and I move swiftly down the hallway to the lounge and watch at the window as he gets into a waiting car. I guess one of his colleagues is picking him up this morning as they are all travelling down by train so that they can work as they go. I trudge back to the kitchen, trying to ignore how empty the house feels all of a sudden. Pulling up the tracking app on my phone as I boil the kettle again, I can see Ben moving away from our road in the direction of town. It gives me a sense of calm when I can visualise where he is, even if I'm just looking at a dot on the screen.

As I pour myself a coffee, having decided tea isn't going to cut it this morning, I check the time to see if it's a reasonable hour to phone Chlo. It's a little early, so I shoot off a text asking her to ring me when she wakes up and take my coffee into the lounge. Unable to bear the quiet, which is ridiculous as he's only been gone a few minutes, I put on the news channel and instantly turn the sound down. Then I pick up my laptop, which I left on the floor, and start to work through my emails and mentally make a to-do list for the day, wanting to complete some tasks before hopefully going away for the weekend.

The morning flies by in a flurry of coffee, biscuits, and work. I'm pretty proud of how much I have achieved but realise around midday that I'm starving. Chlo texted back, saying she'd ring later but that I'd better be coming down today or there would be trouble. The last part made me laugh, and I told her I was but to give me a call with the details of where I'll be staying.

I've been ignoring messages from Charlie all morning, not just because I have work but because I know he is trying to help. He reassured me that I hadn't done or said anything wrong when I was drunk the other night and that he was just concerned about how much I needed to get off of my chest. We apparently had some very drunk, in-depth conversations, and both he and Aiden were worried about me. I know that he is just trying to get me to open up about how I've been feeling, and he has been so supportive over the last few days. Only it's not Charlie I want to sit down and talk to about all this—it's Ben.

I feel more in control than I have done in months. So I leave the texts unanswered. I'll reply tomorrow with a picture of the coast. With that thought in mind, I put down my laptop, go into the kitchen and put on the oven, then go upstairs to pack a bag, taking two stairs at a time. The excitement of going down to see Chloe is bubbling away in my stomach, and I let out a ridiculous "Whoop" when she rings.

"You better be packing, Raz!" Are the first words out of Chloe's mouth as soon as I answer the call.

"Yes, bossy, I am. It's just me, though," I add

"Oh, why? Where's Ben?" She sounds concerned. I hasten to dispel that.

"He has to work in London this weekend, but don't worry. You have me all to yourself." We both chuckle, and I hear a grumpy male voice in the background.

"Tell Marc not to worry. He can have me to himself too." I laugh at my own joke as she relays the message, her laughter is a thing of beauty in my ears, and I make a mental note to make sure I hear a lot of that this weekend.

I walk around the bedroom pulling open drawers and piling clothes onto the bed. It looks like I'm moving out by the time I'm finished. As Chloe tells me to hurry up and pack faster, I use Google Maps to locate the cottage I'll be staying at this weekend. It's one of the rentals next to the pub, belonging to Jay and his family. Just the thought of seeing all of them again puts pep into my step. She starts to tell me all that has been going on, but I cut her off gently.

"You can catch me up on all that later. I'm going to grab some lunch quickly, shower and then head off. I'll text you when I leave. Do you still have that app I asked you to download?" I ask, and she confirms that she does, so I remind her she'll be able to track me, and we end the call.

I race downstairs, grab a sausage roll out of the freezer,

place it on the baking tray in the oven, and dash upstairs again, full of purpose now. I hasten to the shower and get ready in record time, shoving all my clothes and toiletries into a large bag before running downstairs again like a man on a mission because that's what I feel I am. The urgency has taken over, and I need to leave.

As quick as I can, without making myself gag, I chew down the sausage roll and tidy up the kitchen—grab my laptop, chargers and jacket. Then, in a last-minute decision, I search under the stairs in the cupboard to find my walking boots and put those by the door too. Then I'm ready; taking a final look around, I check I haven't left anything on, and then I begin loading the car, which only takes a matter of minutes. Next, I grab my coat; having already placed one jacket in the car, I want to make sure I have enough as the weather looks like it might turn nasty down there over the weekend. Then I lock the door, and I'm in the car with the Sat Nav on and my playlist ready to roll. A quick stop at the local florist to grab a nice bunch for Chlo, and then I'm on the road.

Chapter FOURTEEN

BEN

The train down to London was busy and noisy. We'd booked seats with a table, so half of the team was sat at one table and the other half at another. It worked, sort of, and we managed to get on with a lot of the groundwork we needed for the weekend. There were copious amounts of coffee and some very limp sandwiches from the food carriage, but we made it there in one piece.

Now, as I stand at the window of this standard-sized hotel chain bedroom, I look out over the city and wonder what Raz is doing. He texted before he left Bristol, saying he was heading down to Pendlebrook, but I've not heard from him since. The tracking app he is so fond of tells me he has arrived, but I don't want to bother him if he is reconnecting with Chloe. I don't want to be that boyfriend who bothers the other whilst they are away having fun but equally, I know of Raz's insecurities which have increased tenfold since Chlo was kidnapped so I did text to say I had arrived.

A knock at my hotel door stops my musing, and I let Stu in, grabbing my wallet and room key before we head downstairs to the hotel's restaurant to join the rest of the team for dinner. I'll text Raz later this evening and see how he's doing then, and maybe find out where he is staying too.

We stayed down in the restaurant until the staff started to prepare the other tables for breakfast the following day. It's been fun drinking and chatting out of the office and getting to know some of my colleagues better. Of course, I didn't divulge much about my life; I never do, preferring to keep my home life separate. These aren't real friends; they are acquaintances, and lovely though they are, I don't feel the need to share everything about myself with them.

Once I've returned to the room and got ready for bed, I get comfy and text Raz, not expecting an instant response. He is likely still at the pub. He eventually sent a message that I briefly read when I nipped out to the toilet after dinner. Chlo and Marcus were meeting him at Jay's pub, and that was the last I heard. I expect they were all there, so it's bound to be a late night. Surprisingly three dots appear just as I'm putting the phone down. I browse Instagram whilst I wait, laughing at a photo Chlo has posted of her and Raz sitting at the pub together. The smile on his face is stunning and makes me realise just how long it's been missing.

`Raz: Hey, baby, just back from the pub. I'm staying in one of the cottages next door,` *so not far to stagger, lol. How's the big smoke?*

Even his text sounds cheerful, and I get a pang of nostalgia for how it used to be between us. I miss him, which is ridiculous, but I think it's down to the fact that neither one of us has been ourselves for months, and it's like we are emerging out of a deep dark tunnel. The question is, are we on the same track?

Raz: Want to call?

I tap his number before even consciously thinking about my answer, wanting to hear his voice.

"Hey, baby, you in your room?" he asks as soon as he answers.

"Yes, not long been up here. We had dinner in the restaurant downstairs. How is everyone?" I ask the questions piling out of me, wanting to know everything and experience it with him.

"Amazing. Honestly, I've never seen Chlo happier. She's glowing, and guess who else is glowing?" He hangs out the answer to that, but I know what he is going to say. "Tilly. She looks fantastic, and Connor buzzes around her like a mother hen. It's so funny to watch. Lou and Jay are so damn content it's gorgeous but sickening at the same time."

Raz sighs a sound of contentment and also something else.

"You okay?" I ask. "Sounds like you are having a great time." I make sure that my tone expresses how much joy I find in that, even if I wish I were with him.

"Yeah, it's a lot, you know, being around so many happy, loved up people. Not in a bad way..." he tapers off, and I get a sinking feeling in my stomach. We're happy, aren't we? I mean, it's been a rough few months, but ultimately we are happy, right?

"Why does it sound like you are sad?" I'm not sure what made me ask that.

"I'm not sad, not really. I just wish you were here."

"I wish I were, too, babe." I hear Raz stifle a yawn. "You rest. I bet you have loads planned with Chloe tomorrow. I will be in the office here all day, so I'll text you in the morning and then catch you later in the evening."

"Okay." His voice sounds tired, and I long to be there, holding him in that tiny cottage by the sea.

"Ben?"

"Yes, Raz?"

"I love you."

"Not as much as I love you, though." I laugh as he chuckles on the other end of the phone.

"Get some sleep, okay. I'll speak to you tomorrow," I add, hearing his sleepy reply makes me smile as we disconnect the call.

Despite sounding slightly sad, he also seemed content and more relaxed than I've heard him in a long time. I'm aware that I still haven't managed to have that conversation, and it's getting urgent now as an email arrived today asking me to come for an interview at one of the Cornish firms I applied to. Will he be happy? I hope so.

-

The next day rushes past in a flurry of tube trains, hours spent in the office and a speedy lunch. However, it didn't take us as long as our boss thought it would to complete the task and help our London colleagues finalise the project plans, so between all of us working flat out, we had it finished by the evening. Some of my colleagues chose to stay in London the extra night, but I grabbed a train back to Bristol and booked Monday off work. I'm going to collect my stuff from home and head down to Pendlebrook to surprise Raz. I've already texted Chlo to let her in on the secret because I want to make sure he is there when I arrive.

Raz's texts seem happy enough, but something is missing, like he isn't saying something, and it might be me reading into it too much, so before I make a tit of myself, I intend to go down there and have it out with him once and for all. Lay everything on the table and let him know what I want for our future.

I check in with Mum once I'm on the train home. Jen is doing a bit better now she is away from the house and in the sun. There have been a lot of tears, but that's to be expected. I text Matt, and he confirms he is busy getting Jen's house ready for her to sell. Elle has been over there with Jim and the kids helping out. It's good to see things moving forward there a little, even if it is painful to think about the reason behind it.

Currently, I'm debating whether to turn the tracker off that Raz insists we have on each other at all times. It will ruin the surprise if he knows I'm coming, but I don't want to freak him out if he can't see me. Chloe assured me he hasn't been checking it continuously whilst with her. I gave her a brief rundown of how things had been, but she confirmed that she'd guessed as much from the recent phone calls we'd had and the conversations she has been having with Raz. Chlo said she would try to keep my arrival a secret.

Pulling up the train app, I check the times of the trains and decide that it would be better to leave in the morning rather than journey down tonight, even though there is still no direct train. I would have fewer changes than if I attempted it this late at night. It makes me wonder how Lou managed when she was escaping Damon. I rest my head back against the seat, feeling myself drifting off a little. Worried that I might miss my stop, I shake myself awake, stretching out my legs and arms as much as I can. Temple Meads isn't far now, and I want to grab a taxi home, then I think I'll collapse into bed so I can get up early tomorrow. With that settled, I fire off another text to Chloe to let her know I'll be down by lunch. She agrees to meet me at the station to save me the taxi journey to Pendlebrook.

I've been in our house for five minutes, and I'm feeling shattered. The curtains are closed, and I switch off the kitchen light preparing to head upstairs, when there is a heavy rap at the door. Who the hell is knocking at this time of night?

"Raz? You in there?" A slightly familiar male voice calls through the letterbox, which has just lifted.

I hear a snuffling from the other side of the door and pull it open fast, only to have a huge dog launch itself at me, nearly knocking me over.

"Oh God, I'm so sorry. I thought you weren't here. Your car isn't in the drive. Shit, that sounds bad too. Duke, get down and give the man some air, would you."

Charlie.

I move back out of the doorway, trying to understand why this man is calling looking for my boyfriend at such a ridiculous time of night.

"Raz isn't here." I manage to get the words out, attempting to keep my cool.

Charlie stands there, finally having managed to get the Great Dane to sit down at his feet. He is an incredibly good-looking guy; I'll give Raz that. Lean, tall, dark-haired with a trimmed beard coating his jaw.

"I see that now. I'm so sorry. I've just finished my shift, and I needed to walk Duke, so I thought we would drop by. I saw the light on," he rambles. A look of embarrassment crosses his face, but then it's gone. "So he's okay?"

"I'm not sure why you are standing on my doorstep at this time of night asking whether *my* boyfriend is okay, but yes, Raz is fine, thank you. So, you can go now." My harsh tone shocks me a little. I'm not usually this dismissive of other people, but I'm tired, and this good-looking man asking about my boyfriend has pissed me off.

"Right. Yes, I suppose it would look a little weird to you."

His statement gets my back up, and I'm about to tell him where to go when the dog decides to step into the house and nuzzle at my hand, whining at me and giving me the look. *You know the one dogs get when they are trying to convey something to you, but you haven't got a clue what they want.*

"Sorry, he senses your distress. Probably anger. God knows I'd feel annoyed if some guy turned up on my doorstep asking about my husband."

His what now?

"I haven't even introduced myself properly. My manners are appalling, sorry. I'll blame it on a long shift and the time of night." He stretches his hand towards me, and I swear my jaw hasn't left the floor yet. On autopilot, I shake his hand. "My name's Charlie, and this is Duke. We met Raz in the park around the corner a week or so ago. I'm not great with time, but I've known him a short while. Damn, I'm rambling."

His skin is soft against mine, and I let his hand go, dropping mine at my side. Then step back from the door a little more and gesture them both inside.

"Are you sure? It's very late," Charlie says but steps over the threshold anyway, and Duke starts to look around, giving everything a good sniff as we stand awkwardly in the hall. I shut the door and stretch my arm out towards the lounge.

"Have a seat. Now tell me more about how you bumped into my boyfriend at the park." It's time I got answers.

So he explains how Duke is sensitive to emotions. Even from a distance, he could tell Raz was upset and took it upon himself to make that better. We both laugh as Duke now sits next to me on the floor with his head in my lap. I've taken one of the sofa chairs whilst Charlie sits at the other end of the sofa, with Duke's lead in his hand.

"I could see he wasn't in a good place. I'm a nurse," he says by way of an explanation. "I work with end-of-life patients and their families. I also volunteer part-time with the Samaritans."

I nod and get up briefly, grabbing us both a beer from the fridge because I think we need it.

"Raz looked so lost, and I wasn't sure that he should be on his own, so we got a coffee. He told me a bit about his friend and about you. I'm so sorry for your loss." Charlie seems genuine in his concern, and it's clear that Raz has been talking to him quite a bit.

"I just wanted to provide him with someone to talk to, but honestly, he's a great guy, and we seemed to hit it off."

Something must show on my face as Duke nuzzles me, and Charlie holds up a hand towards me.

"Nothing like that, I can assure you. I'm very much in love with my husband, but I enjoyed spending time with Raz, and so did Aiden. That's my husband. He came out with us the other night when Raz had a bit too much to drink," Charlie explains, and I laugh at the understatement.

"He was shitfaced, you mean." I chuckle, and Charlie smiles at me.

"Yeah. I guess Raz doesn't usually drink much? I didn't realise."

"It's fine. More like, we haven't drunk much over the last few months. It's been a very dark hole that we got ourselves into. Surviving each day at a time..." I've probably said too much; damn, this man is easy to talk to.

"I got that impression. When he didn't answer my messages yesterday and today, I got worried. Stupid really. I don't know him from Adam, but I just wanted to check he hadn't got himself lost again."

"I'm sure he will be sorry to have worried you. He's with Chloe in Cornwall, and honestly, when those two are together, they can forget the rest of the world." A chuckle pulls itself out of me as I think of how little Raz has texted me today.

"Does that bother you?" Charlie asks, his eyes seeming interested and not at all judgmental.

"In the beginning, I thought there was something in it, but there isn't. Raz and Chloe have been together since they were kids, and they were all each other had for a long time,"

I explain, although I'm not sure why I feel I need to.

"When she was kidnapped and tortured, Raz blamed himself. He hasn't forgiven himself yet, and with all that I've been dealing with, the loss of my nephew and ex-brother-in-law. Well, I haven't exactly been that supportive," I admit thinking back over the last few months about the amount of time I've left Raz to go and stay with my sister.

"It's odd because Raz said the same thing."

I look at Charlie, bemused and a little upset that Raz would be blaming me for abandoning him, even if I've just admitted to feeling as though I have to a complete stranger.

"He feels guilty that he wasn't there for you enough," Charlie clarifies, and the pieces all start to fall into place.

"Anyway, thank you for the beer and Duke thanks you for the head rubs. I'd best be off, or Aiden will call the police."

I join in Charlie's laughter as he gets up and whistles for Duke to come with him. Reluctantly the dog leaves my side after another tickle behind the ears.

"Your husband sounds a lot like Raz."

"Yes, I suppose they are a little similar. I'm glad he's okay. Aiden will be, too. He's been flapping a little, so at least I can put his mind at rest," Charlie says as he makes his way to the front door.

"It was nice to finally meet you properly. I hope we can all get together sometime, maybe grab a drink or a bite to eat?"

It's weird because I would have declined this man's

offer an hour ago, but after spending just a few minutes in his company, I can see why Raz likes him. I readily agree to meet up as I see him out and lock the door behind them. A sense of relief has settled over me, and now that I know who Charlie is and why he has been concerned about my boyfriend. I feel even more sure that Raz and I need to clear the air.

Chapter FIFTEEN

RAZ

I'm not going to lie; I love it here. And being away from Bristol has given me more clarity—as if I needed it—about what I want in life. Now all I need to do is persuade Ben that moving down here would be a good idea. I'm just worried that he won't agree. His family is there, and now, after all that's happened with Jen this year, he might not want to move that far away. Then there is his job, and even though I don't think he loves the work he does, how can I ask him to just give it up?

"Raz, you decent?" Chloe's voice and the creak of the front door have me looking over from my position in the kitchen.

"Bit late if I wasn't." I laugh at her as she just lets herself in regardless. I've missed this.

"Yeah, well, I've seen it all before. I just wanted to give you a chance to put something on, but I see you're dressed already." Her smile warms my heart, and I find that I'm able to breathe better. Just seeing how happy she is here with Marcus and all the others in the life she is carving out for herself. It makes me so damn ecstatic and finally takes away some of the guilt I've been feeling. I may also have got a little tipsy last night and had a heart to heart with her and Marc, who came and joined us after work. He is the best thing that could have happened to Chlo, and seeing them together makes me a little sad that Ben isn't with me to share this experience, to see just how happy she is and how good life down here could be.

"I thought I'd get ready early. What are we up to today?" I ask, gesturing to the kettle to ask if she wants a drink.

"About that, I'm going to ask for a raincheck this morning. I just need to pop out and get something around lunchtime," she says, looking cagey like she's hiding something, but I let it slide.

"Okay, that's fine. I'll go for a bit of a walk, get some sea air and meet you later? Tea? Coffee?"

"Yes, coffee, please, and that's a great idea. I won't be too long. I'll text you when I'm back." Chloe beams at me and sits down on the high stool at the kitchen counter. I love this little cottage, and I can just see Ben and me in one like this. With an open fire in the lounge for the brutal winters and a little courtyard garden out the back to sit in during the summer.

"It's not supposed to rain this morning, but the weather might turn nasty later, so be prepared." Chloe laughs at me as I turn around cocking an eyebrow at her.

"Yes, Mum!"

I try to keep my face serious, but it's impossible as she starts waggling her eyebrows at me. A big belly laugh erupts from me, it feels so damn good, but once I start, I just can't stop. Bending over double, I try to contain myself, but tears stream down my face as all the emotion I thought I'd kept in check leaks out of my eyes at the relief of being able to laugh again.

"Oh, Raz," Chlo's voice startles me; I hadn't realised she'd moved and was standing right beside me. The gentle touch of her hand on my back is my undoing, and I find myself sobbing into her shoulder as she rubs my back to comfort me.

Finally, I'm able to breathe again; I feel drained but also more myself.

"Chlo. I'm..."

"Don't you dare apologise for being emotional, Raz. You know we don't do that. Not now and not ever." She gently scolds me whilst manoeuvring my body towards a stool, and I gladly sit down and look at her, wiping the back of my hand across my eyes. "It's okay to let it out. You don't have to keep your feelings hidden. Especially not around me."

Damn, she knows me; even now, after all she has been

through, she's the one comforting me. I shake my head at the thought.

"Look at me, Raz. I'm fine. I honestly am. Yes, it took some time, but I'm better now, I promise." She starts to fill two mugs with hot water as I check her over; I'm not sure what for, but as she bustles around the light and airy kitchen making coffee dressed in a hoodie and jeans, I can see just how fine she is now. Sure she has scars, they will always be there, and I know she will probably hide them sometimes, but Chloe is okay. It's about time I moved forward too.

"You're right. I know I need to let it out and not hold my emotions in. I'm trying to be better at doing that because it's been eating me alive."

"You've nothing to feel guilty about, Raz. We discussed this last night. What happened to me was not your fault." She places a cup of coffee in front of me and perches on the stool next to mine. Reaching out, Chloe squeezes my hand.

"Being down here, seeing you again and how good you look now. It's helping." I feel my lips start to lift in a smile as I leave my hand entwined with hers. "I've missed you, Chlo."

"Yeah, that is the one thing I wish was different. I love this place, and I can't imagine ever leaving here now. I just wish you and Ben were here too." She grins at me and lets go of my hand, picking her mug up and cradling it between her fingers before blowing a little and then taking a sip.

"I'd love that too. I'm just not sure if Ben would agree to the move. His work and family are all in Bristol. It's not so easy for him to relocate. If it were just me, I would be here in a heartbeat." I look around the quaint cottage kitchen area and back at Chloe. "I could live in a place like this," I add as I pick up my mug and enjoy a tentative sip of the hot, bitter liquid.

"If this is really where your heart is, then maybe have a conversation with Ben about it. If this year has taught us anything, it's that life is for living. We can't be scared to take a risk, and we certainly need to move forwards and not stagnate." She takes another sip of her coffee before adding, "Now come closer and take a look over this plan I have for Tilly's baby shower. Lou and I want to throw her an intimate but fun celebration." Chloe pulls out her phone, and after tapping at her notes, she thrusts it towards me.

We spend an hour or so going over her plans and ordering a couple of presents. One from Ben and me and another from her and Marcus. It feels comfortable and real. All too soon, she is getting up to leave, but I don't get a panicked feeling; it just feels natural.

"It looks nice out still. Bloody cold, but at least it's not raining." Chloe looks over her shoulder at me as she opens the wooden front door and starts to walk out. I nod my agreement, saying goodbye and see you later.

Once alone, I wash up our mugs and tidy the kitchen a little. Then pull out my phone to plan my route. Deciding on a mix of coastal path and beach walking, I pull on a lightweight jacket over my hoodie; just in case it rains, it will offer a little protection whilst I run back here. Finally, I pull on my walking boots, grab my headphones and lock up.

The sun is making a weak attempt at an appearance and still holds a little strength in its glare, but summer is far behind us now, and autumn has us in her blustery grip speeding us into winter. It's far colder than I imagined by the ocean, and as I make my way across the beach, I hope that walking at a fast pace will warm me up. Over by the shoreline, I see a young mother dashing after her toddler, trying to keep her away from the water as she calls her name repeatedly. The sweet little blonde-haired girl, Cally, I think I heard her mum call her, laughs in abandon as she heads towards the sea again. A smile breaks out across my lips as I take a deep inhale of the salty sea air. This is bliss.

I'll check in with Ben once I get back, I think as I take large strides across the sand and reach the path that winds up the hill on the other side. Music plays softly in my ears, but I decide to take my headphones out as the wind has picked up, and I'd rather listen to the sound of the crashing waves and the seagulls crying overhead, living in the moment, experiencing it all—the sights, the sounds, and the smells. I nod a greeting to the occasional walker as I make my way further over the cliffs and down the other side. There is a slight dip here and what looks like an overgrown path down to the little private beach, as I can only see a sliver from up here. I decide to go and investigate. This might be a perfect place for Ben and me to come for a picnic in the summer.

Halfway down, I realise my mistake. The path isn't really a path, maybe a worn animal track? It's a bit of a climb in places and definitely not worth bringing Ben to. It might be better reached by boat perhaps. Deciding I had better turn back, as I'm sure I felt a spot of rain then, and the sky overhead had become darker whilst I was concentrating on navigating my way down here. I pull out my phone to take a quick picture and nearly drop it. I overreach to stop it from falling and miss my footing. It all happens so quickly; one minute, I'm on the path, a little close to the rocky edge and the next, I'm tumbling downwards with a death grip on my phone. The pain as I hit my body on jagged rocks heightens the fright shooting through me, causing me to yell out. Then everything goes black.

The sound of moaning and water close by rouses me. It takes me a moment to register that I'm not in bed. My body aches and my head is pounding. I force my eyelids to open, squinting against the pain and the raindrops assaulting my eyes. I turn my head gently to the side to assess the situation. It's not good.

From my upside-down vantage point, I can see there was no way, as I had begun to suspect, that I would ever have made it to the tiny beach from above. The rocky cliffs surrounding it are sheer drops of jagged black rocks, broken up with the odd tuft of grass or little ledge. Turning my head the other way, I assess that I'm at the bottom of one such cliff, and I've landed awkwardly on some rocks which jut out from where there was once sand, I suspect, but now to my horror, I notice the water. The sea is very close, so close that I can feel the spray on my face mingling with the rain from above. For a few seconds, blind panic washes over me and I scream for help. Will anyone be up on the cliff now that it's raining? Will they even hear me over the roar of the waves crashing against the rocks close by?

Think, Raz! I need to get myself upright a little if I can. It's painful to move, but I want to do it anyway, even though my head is telling me I probably shouldn't move too much in case I've seriously damaged something. I start off small by checking in with my legs and arms to see if I can feel them. I can certainly feel the pain that radiates through my right leg and in my left arm, which seems to be at a funny angle. Fuck. Then I hear a buzzing sound; it's out of place against the backdrop of rushing water and seagulls. *Is that my phone?*

Chapter SIXTEEN

BEN

The whole journey down, I expect Raz to message or ring me asking why I'm not in London. The excitement builds the closer I get to Cornwall, and I can't wait to get off the train. It's been hours since I caught a taxi to the station with my small suitcase full of clothes. I've packed some for my interview on Tuesday and organised more time off from work. My boss wasn't all that happy about the extra day I wanted, but he conceded that we managed to complete the difficult task in London in record time. It was a short email exchange as it's the weekend. I didn't want a long, drawn-out discussion about a few days off. I rarely take time off, and I have holiday owing.

I made sure to let Mum and Dad know where I was going, not wanting to cause the family worry if they couldn't get hold of me as the mobile service down in Cornwall can be spotty, and I don't want to be on the phone much. No, I intend to spend every moment I can with Raz convincing him that we can move down to Cornwall. It's a rash decision, I know, but I just want more out of life; plus, there is something I need to ask him, and it's not going to wait any longer. I need to know.

As I disembark the last train and step out onto the platform, I hear a female voice I recognise calling my name. Looking around, I see Chloe walking at speed toward me; I just have time to let go of my suitcase before she launches herself into my arms.

"Ben, I'm so glad you're here. I've missed you." Her words are genuine and a sentiment I share. I hadn't realised until this moment just how much I've missed having her around.

"Hey, Chlo, I've missed you too." I chuckle, untangling myself from her hug to get a good look at her. "You look fantastic." And it's true she looks so much better than when we moved her down from Bristol, and even then, she was improving from the almost catatonic state she had been in after the kidnapping.

"Did we manage to keep it a surprise?" I ask, looking around, sure that Raz would be with her if he knew I was coming. I pull at the handle of my wheeled suitcase, getting it ready to drag behind me.

"Yes, he has no idea. I kept him busy this morning, and now he's gone for a short walk. Although," —she looks up at the sky as we start to walk away from the platform and out of the station— "It looks like it's about to rain, so he'll probably be heading back soon. We might not make it to the cottage before he gets there." She looks thoughtful. Then links her arm in mine as we head towards the car park.

The drive down the winding country lanes feels like coming home, and I lay out my thoughts to Chlo to see what she thinks. Having made the move herself, I want to know if it is all I've hyped it up in my head to be.

"I think Raz is on the same page, Ben. Honestly, I do. He looks so damn relaxed down here and even said this morning that he could live in a cottage like the one he is renting. So I'd say you won't have to persuade him much." The huge grin on her face pulls an answering one from my lips, and I feel the anticipation of seeing my boyfriend and approaching this next chapter of our life together bubbling away in my stomach.

We park in the pub car park and walk the short distance to the cottage. It looks so quaint from the outside, all white stone and blue-edged windows with a blue wooden door. I can see why Raz loves it, but he doesn't appear to be here, though.

"Well, that's weird. Maybe he went further than he planned and is still on his way back?" Chloe suggests as we try knocking at that door but get no answer. "I'll go get the spare key from Jay. Do you want to come over to the pub out of the rain for a bit?"

"Sure," I say, not wanting to stand out in this weather

for too long. It's not raining hard, but the sky overhead suggests that it could get worse.

The inside of the pub isn't busy, but I can see a few people who have clearly taken shelter from the rain and are nursing a steaming mug of coffee and a plate of cake. Deciding that I could do the same, I walk up to the bar with Chloe and greet Jay. He bustles about behind the bar, calling down the corridor to Lou, who appears as if by magic from the back and comes around the side of the bar. I accept the hug she offers and sit down on a stool with her and Chloe as we catch up. It feels so right, so natural, the stress of the last few weeks evaporates as we talk, and I breathe a sigh of relief at being home—that's how it feels to me.

Coffee appears in front of me as if Jay could read my mind, and I thank him and let their conversation drift over me as I pull out my phone, beginning to worry that Raz isn't back now. Looking out of the small wooden framed pub window, I see that the rain has picked up. Silly to worry that he's getting wet, but I just want him here, in my arms.

I sip on my coffee and pull up the app, watching as his dot appears on the map. It seems to be in the sea, which makes me chuckle. If there is one thing Raz won't be doing right now, it's swimming, especially around this coast in the autumn. As I watch, expecting it to start moving back towards town as he's likely on the coastal path, I sip my coffee, stopping to add a sugar cube from the little pot Jay just put in front of me. I stir, again looking at the dot, but it's not moving. Something doesn't feel right. Maybe I'm just anxious to see him after chatting with Charlie and travelling down here.

"You okay, Ben?" Chloe stops talking to Lou and Jay and looks at me. I glance up from my vigil on the phone and try to decide if I'm being stupid or if I should say something. "Raz will be back any minute, I'm sure," she adds, squeezing my hand, which is resting on the bar by my coffee cup.

"You're right. I'm just feeling tired, I'm sure, but I can't shake this weird feeling. He doesn't appear to be moving on the app." I release a breath feeling a little silly that I voiced my concerns. Raz is a grown man, for goodness sake.

"I've texted him, but he hasn't replied." A look of doubt crosses her face, and I hasten to reassure her as well as myself.

"He probably has his phone in his pocket and hasn't looked at it," I state, looking back at my own phone.

"If you are worried, why doesn't Chlo ring him and see where he is?" Lou asks, reaching for a packet of crisps across the bar. Jay gets there first and places an assortment in front of her as they share a sickeningly sweet look that makes my lips twitch. I'd smile if I weren't beginning to get a horrible feeling something's wrong.

"Good plan. I'll just tell him I'm back and that we have plans this afternoon, so he needs to get a shift on and come to the pub for lunch." Chloe gets up and fishes her phone out of her back pocket. Sitting down on the stool next to me again, she presses Raz's contact details and puts the mobile to her ear.

It just rings.

"Maybe he just can't hear it over the wind?" Chloe suggests ending the call that went to voicemail without leaving a message. "It gets extremely windy on the coastal path this time of year." She looks to Lou for reassurance.

"It does. Has the dot moved on your app, Ben? I'm wondering if maybe the weather is interfering with it?" Lou asks me, and I look down at my phone again, waking it up and refreshing the app. It hasn't moved, so I shake my head to let them know.

"What's going on?" Jay asks as he comes back from serving a customer and looks at us all just sitting there.

"Raz isn't back yet; he isn't answering his phone, and Ben's app suggests he hasn't moved since Ben got here, which is over half an hour ago," Lou sums it up, looking at her watch to check the time.

"I'm sure he's fine. He just hasn't heard his phone. Why not try again," Jay suggests reaching across the bar and rubbing Lou's arm a little as he reassures her.

Chloe picks up her phone and tries again. It rings for what seems like an eternity, and I'm sure it will go to voicemail again, then the line crackles so much I can hear it from here.

"Raz? Raz, can you hear me?" Chloe shouts down the phone. There is a lot of what sounds like water, maybe the sea? Is he still on the cliffs?

"Raz, don't move!" Chloe yells and grabs my hand; that's when I realise my feeling of foreboding wasn't off. Something is dreadfully wrong with my boyfriend, and the tears appearing at the corners of Chlo's eyes confirm it. Lou and Jay stop what they are doing and edge closer. Chlo gets up off the stool, and I put my arm around her, still not sure what's happening but feeling that I need to comfort her.

"Ben's here, I'm going to put him on in a second whilst I get you help. Okay? You just stay awake." Her hand shakes as she turns to me with her phone. Jay has already picked up his.

"Call the coastguard, Jay. Raz has fallen over a cliff, and the tide is coming in on him." Chloe turns to me, taking my phone out of my hand and giving it to Lou so they can confirm my boyfriend's location, I assume. I don't know because all I can hear is Chlo's words on repeat in my brain, Raz has fallen over a cliff, and the tide is coming in.

"He can't swim very well." I don't know why those words come out of my mouth, but they do, and the sob that comes from Chlo makes me shake myself out of the shock I'm in. I pick up her phone and place it by my ear.

"Babe, you there?" I ask, hoping to hear his cheery voice telling me it's all going to be okay, but all I get is a groan.

"Ben? Is that you? I'm sorry, baby. I'm so sorry." His voice seems far away, and I can barely make out his words. Chloe is pulling me towards the back of the pub, and I follow her blindly into a little office and let her push me gently into a chair. The lack of noise in this area of the pub just makes the sound of the waves and wind more evident on the other end of the phone.

"Babe, what happened? Are you okay? You have nothing to be sorry for." My words are all jumbled as I try to make sense of this situation which is feeling more and more surreal by the minute.

"I fell. I was trying to find us a nice cove to have a picnic. I wanted to bring you down here for the weekend." His voice trails off, and he breathes heavily into the phone.

"Don't try and talk, babe, just listen, okay. I'm here right now, waiting to spend a few days with you down here. So, I need you to be okay. We have so much that we need to discuss." I know I'm rambling, but it feels good to get it out there, to hear him breathing in my ear even though he sounds like he is in pain.

"I think I've broken my arm, and I can't really move." He starts to moan a little as if he is attempting to move.

"Don't move!" I shout down the phone, thinking of all the injuries he could have after a fall like that. Chloe moves in closer, and I tuck her under my arm. I forgot she was here with me.

"I'm going to go and find out what's happening," Chlo whispers from beside me. I give her a quick squeeze and a nod as she turns and leaves the room shutting the door behind her.

"Raz? You still with me?" I ask as I can't hear him for a second.

"Yeah, just trying to keep away from the water; it's bloody cold." He tries a half chuckle but moans instead.

"Stay calm, babe. Help is on the way. They'll find you, and then we can spend some time down here just chilling out. I've got so much I want to say." I add the last part trying to hold back from asking him the most important thing on the phone whilst he's hurting and in danger. Then he starts to cough and splutter.

"The water is coming in fast, Ben. I... I... don't think they will get here in time." His tone is so apologetic and sad that my heart breaks a little, but I refuse to believe it is going to end like this.

"No, you stay strong. Do you hear me? Fight, Raz. I won't let you go like this. This is not the end for us. You are my everything, do you understand..." There is no response.

"Raz, babe, please, hold on. I want you to be my husband. Do you hear me? Raz!"

Chapter SEVENTEEN

RAZ

I swear I'm getting delirious; they say that about swallowing salt water, don't they? I try to move my head a little further away from the waves that are creeping ever closer. The spray is in my mouth, my eyes, and one ear is definitely full of water, and to the other, I'm holding my phone so tight that I'm not sure I just heard my boyfriend correctly. *Did he just ask me to marry him?*

"Marry me," he whispers, and I know that I heard him right that time.

There is a low droning sound out on the water, and I gently turn my head to see the beautiful sight of an RNLI lifeboat getting closer. I don't know if they will get me out of the water in time, and as another wave reaches me, I hold my breath, trying not to let the spray overtake me.

"YES!" I shout the word down my phone, hoping it's still working. It is waterproof, but I've never tested it. Never had cause to. A sob on the other end of the phone sounds like Chloe, and I hear her question Ben whether he asked me to marry him. He confirms he did.

"This is not how I wanted to ask you. I was going to see how you felt about our future. Find out what you were thinking. I planned a whole proper proposal, but I can't wait another second." Ben's voice is loud and clear. It's all I'm hearing as I try to zone out and not let the panic overcome me as the water begins to lap at my face, and with each wave that enters the cove, it covers my left arm, which I'm convinced is broken. I've landed in such a strange position; I must have tumbled about a lot after hitting my head. Last I checked, that was still bleeding too.

"Raz?"

I think I spaced out a little there; I heard my name being called, and I couldn't decide if it was on the phone or close by.

"Raz. We've got you. Stay with us. We're going to get you out of here." A strong, determined tone has me blinking to my left and trying to see through the water. "Try not to move. I'm just going to put this collar on you, and we'll get you on the stretcher in just a second. Let's make this assessment quick. We don't have much time."

"Connor?" I ask, finally linking the voice to the man.

"Yes. I'm here, Raz. It's going to be okay. Let me take your phone. I'll put it in my pocket." He reaches over, but before he takes it, I need to let Ben know.

"I love you, baby. You are it for me too. I can't wait to marry you." I hear Ben inhale sharply as I end the call and hand my phone over to Connor.

There are a couple of them here now, only I can't see them all as I've been fitted with a cervical collar, or so I'm told as they give me a full-body assessment as quickly as they can, asking me all sorts of questions as they start stabilising parts of my body to move me onto a spine board. But unfortunately, I'm not paying proper attention as the water is sending me into a panic as it gets closer and closer.

"Focus on my voice. Breathe in and out slowly, Raz. We'll have you out of here in a second."

A loud noise overhead alerts me to the presence of a helicopter, and I'm shielded from the downdraft by Connor as he leans over me. They managed to move me on the board a bit further up the rocks and out of the water, but he explained that they didn't want to jolt me around on the boat in case I've injured my spine.

He introduces me to the paramedic from the helicopter, who appears in my line of vision fully kitted up with a helmet on. The man has a kind, caring face as he tells me what is about to happen.

"I'll let the others know what's going on once I'm back at the station, then we'll get Ben to the hospital." Connor gives me a gentle squeeze on my good arm as the stretcher I'm on begins to lift into the air with Jon, the kind-looking guy from the helicopter, at my side.

"I'm getting married," I say for no apparent reason once we are securely inside the helicopter and I've opened my eyes again. I couldn't cope with the feeling of being pulled up through the air, so I shut it out.

"Well, we'd best get you back to the hospital so they can fix you up then, hadn't we." Jon's West Country accent washes over me, bringing a sense of calm. Or that might be the painkillers he's currently administering.

"I like your tattoos. I think I should get one." Okay, I need to shut up now, but I'm reassured by the chuckle that comes from Jon that it's alright that I'm a little off my head on pain medication.

I've never been in a helicopter before, and I'm a little sad that I don't get to see the view from up here, but wow, the noise is incredible. Jon asks questions every now and then. Not letting me fall asleep the way I want to, but I get it, I've got a head injury, and they need to check that out. At least the pain in the rest of my body has subsided. I wonder where Ben is. Did he hear me say yes? I think he did. It's hard to remember what is real and what isn't right now.

Jon's voice is close to me again, telling me we are landing in a few minutes and that the hospital staff are waiting for us on the helicopter pad, which is on the roof of the hospital. I try to think of the geography of Cornwall and where the hospital is in relation to Pendlebrook, but my mind won't cooperate.

The bleeping of machinery and bright lights startle me

as I come out of the haze again, words are being fired around, but I can't grasp them. What did they say they were going to do? Jon appears briefly in my line of sight to say that he is heading back out on another call and that the hospital staff will take it from here. Another face takes his place as I try to say thank you to him.

"Hi there, Raz. I'm Doctor Forestman. Do you know where you are?" Why is he asking that? Of course, I know where I am.

I try to reply, but for some reason, the words don't want to form.

"We will need to take you for a CT scan and X-rays," he says, his face close to mine as he shines a light in my eyes. Those pain meds are making me sleepy, but they won't let me sleep, their questions are giving me a headache, and those lights are too bright. Did I just moan?

How many hours have I been here? The tests are never-ending as the nurses and doctors flit around me. I was moved from the helicopter stretcher when I arrived, I think. I've been in and out of machines, and casts have been placed on my leg and arm. Now I'm finally in a bed which is at the end of a room of about six beds. Mine is fortunately near the window.

It turns out I was pretty lucky even though I feel like I've been through a washing cycle on high spin. No spinal damage, and although my head was injured and I'm being kept in for observation, my brain seems to be fine. Well, as fine as it ever was, I joked with the nurse, and she gave me a smile. These pain meds are fantastic. One broken wrist, a few bruised ribs and a fractured Tibia in my right leg. Other than that, there are plenty of scrapes and bruises, which they cleaned and dressed for me. My leg and arm are in plaster, making moving about difficult, but the smiley nurse put the button close to my hand so I could call for assistance if I needed it.

I'm hoping that now I'm settled here, they will let me see Ben. I know he's here because the doctor told me my fiancée is here. That made me smile. I guess he did hear me say yes.

"Raz? Oh God, babe." Ben's voice startles me a little as he enters the room and rushes toward me. The nurse who must have shown him in pulls the curtain between my bed and the next, giving us some privacy.

Ben's face is pale and drawn with an expression of horror and concern written all over it as his eyes check me over. Then he drags a chair over to sit next to the bed. I reach over to him with my good hand and immediately feel the warmth of his touch as our skin connects.

"Hey," I manage, trying to stop the tears that have formed in the corner of my eyes from falling. I'm feeling way too emotional right now. Ben gently pulls my hand to his lips and kisses my knuckles.

"Don't ever scare me like that again. Raz, I thought…" He turns away, hiding his face, but I didn't miss the look of pain in his eyes.

"It's okay, Ben, I'm fine. A little bashed up, but I'm okay, I promise." I try to pull him back to me but wince as the movement pulls on my ribs.

"Are you in pain? Should I get someone?" Ben turns back at my attempt to pull him closer and goes into full flap mode.

"Ben, shhh, I'm okay. Just pulled on my ribs a bit. I'm going to need a bit of help when they let me out of here," I admit, not loving the idea, but it's best to get that out in the open now.

"Whatever you need." He nods before looking at me with a serious expression. "I meant what I said, Raz. I want to marry you. I'll take you in sickness and in health and everything in between. You are mine. My everything, my future…" His voice falters, and I see the emotion he is trying to hold on to shining as tiny droplets form in his eyes.

"Baby, I am yours. I always have been, as you are mine. From the moment we met, I have never wanted another man as much as I want you every damn time I look at you. I love you with every part of me, and yes, I will marry you." I needed to confirm that, not just for Ben but for me too. This is a massive step for me, and I'm willing to take it with him. To spend the rest of my life with Ben by my side. My lips pull up in a huge grin as he leans forward and kisses me gently on the forehead.

"Thank God. I thought I misheard you." He chuckles,

clearly relieved that I had said yes. "I had a full speech prepared to convince you that marrying me was a good idea."

I try not to laugh as it hurts, "A good idea, hey?"

"The best." He confirms with a nod as he sits back down next to the bed and strokes my knuckles with his thumb.

We sit in comfortable silence for a second, and then Ben tells me about Charlie's late-night visit and their discussion.

"I'm ashamed to admit I was a little jealous of him. I thought you had grown tired of me." His confession shocks me a little.

"Why, Ben? When have I ever given you the impression that I've had enough?" I feel a bit hurt at the suggestion. I know I've been in a dark place, but I don't think I gave off the vibe of being tired of the one person who has kept me sane through all of this.

"It was me and my insecurities, babe, not you. We've both had so much to deal with, and I think we lost ourselves somewhere along the way." Ben shrugs, and I can see how tired he is from the dark circles under his eyes.

"We need to communicate more. I'm willing to admit I haven't been the best at it," I state as he shakes his head, trying to deny my words even though we both know it's true.

"There is something else. Something I've been kind of keeping from you because I wasn't sure if it would pan out."

Oh crap, I'm not sure my heart can take much more right now.

A BRIDGE TO FOREVER

"I want to move to Cornwall."

Okay, I wasn't expecting that.

Chapter EIGHTEEN

BEN

Although Connor had given us a fair idea of what happened, nothing prepared me for actually seeing the love of my life bandaged up, covered in cuts and bruises and hooked up to machines and an IV in a hospital bed. I had to turn away when it got too much. I didn't want him to see how scared I'd been that I'd lost him for good.

Then it was like a dam broke; I had to get it all out, every thought, every feeling. I probably should have waited a bit because he's looking at me in total shock.

"You want to move here?" he asks, his tone disbelieving.

"Yes, I applied for a few jobs, not knowing if I would get them or not. I'm not happy at work, Raz. I haven't been for some time."

"Why didn't you say something?" Raz looks stunned. Fuck, I should have waited; this is too much too soon, maybe.

"It never seemed like the time was right, and I thought I could just plough through it, but I can't. I need a change, and what better place to start that than here?" I try to make him understand.

"You mean it?" he asks, his eyes squint a little as he tries to read me.

"Yes, I want to do this now. There are no guarantees in life, and we don't know what's around the corner. Why wait? I think we both need a change of scenery. What do you say?"

Raz shakes his head a little, and I think he will suggest I'm insane. "I was wondering how to convince you to move down here, and all the time you wanted to anyway." He chuckles and winces a little making me grip his hand a little tighter. Does he mean what I think he does?

"Let's do it. If you're sure this is what you want because I'm all in for a move down here." His bruised and battered face beams with delight at the idea, and relief floods me with his words.

"Thank goodness because I've got an interview on Tuesday and I really want the job. It's a change of pace and fewer hours, but I think we can make it work." I know I'm rambling, but I'm so excited to finally have a chance to discuss my plans with Raz.

"You have an interview?" His voice raises a little in surprise, and a laugh escapes me at the look on his face.

"We have a lot of plans to make," I confirm, feeling a

little excited for this new chapter in our lives. First, though, we need to get Raz on the mend and what better place to do that than here in Cornwall. Jay has said we could stay in the cottage for the next few weeks. Which when I tell Raz seems to make him really happy. I pull up a couple of estate agents' sites on my phone, and we sit and look through the cottages available. There aren't many, and prices in Pendlebrook and the surrounding area are quite high, but I've got Chloe on the case now as I shot her off a quick text when the nurse came in to check on Raz. Visiting hours are coming to an end, and I'm reluctant to leave him here, but after a quick discussion with his doctor, who confirms Raz should be out tomorrow, I head off, promising to return in the morning.

Chloe is outside waiting for me when I exit the hospital into the dark night, the air is cold, and I pull my jacket around me tightly. Chlo has Raz's phone, so I run back in and ask reception if they can make sure he gets it. They assured me he would. At least now Raz will be able to text; Chlo charged it on her way over with her in-car charger.

"How is he?" Chlo asks, her face showing her anxiety, and I give her hand a gentle squeeze as I reassure her that he's doing okay.

"Thank goodness. I hope you told him how much he scared us all!" She jokes, but I can see she's serious as we exit the car park and head back to Pendlebrook. "Marc has finished work and will meet us at the pub, and Jay saved some food for you." She continues to chat with me as she navigates the roads expertly.

"I grabbed the keys to the cottage and Raz's things," I say, finally getting a word in and shaking the plastic bag I placed in the footwell when I got in the car. Unfortunately, his clothes couldn't be saved, so I'll need to bring more in tomorrow, and I make a mental note to bring joggers, not jeans, so that we can get them over his leg plaster.

I spend the rest of the journey talking about our plans. Chloe is ecstatic that we intend to move down here and has already made a shortlist of properties we should look at. Some aren't even on the market yet. However, she knows they are ready to sell through word of mouth. We get caught up in the excitement as we talk about all the pros and cons of the properties she's looked at, and we arrive back at the pub in no time.

My evening was cosy, that's how I would describe it. The warmth of the open fire in the pub, the tasty meal that Jay saved for me, and the company was all wonderfully familiar. Tilly and Connor only stayed briefly, but long enough for Connor explain how close I came to losing Raz.

I let myself into the cottage. It's not too late but already pitch-black outside. The sound of the boats moving around in the harbour travels to me on the wind, pulling a tired smile to my lips. Inside the cottage, it's dark but thankfully warm. Jay popped in whilst I was in the hospital and put the heating on when he dropped my suitcase off earlier. I remind myself to thank him again for doing that.

Flicking the light switch on by the front door, I get my first look at the little cottage, which will be home for the week. I will be speaking to my boss tomorrow and telling him what happened. There is no way I'm leaving Raz down here by himself these next few weeks.

My suitcase is in the hallway waiting for me, so I take my shoes off, lock up, and then walk through into the little lounge area. The log burner is ready to use, but I'll save that until Raz and I are cuddled up on the rather comfy looking dark blue sofa. Raz's laptop is here, and I look around for his charger. Finding it plugged in by the TV, I put the laptop on charge, knowing he will want that when he gets back.

Once I illuminate the kitchen with the under-cabinet lights, I get the full feeling of coming home. I can see why Raz liked this place. It's not very big, but it's perfect for us. There is a courtyard out the back, or so I'm told, but I can't see it as it's too dark outside, two bedrooms and a bathroom, a kitchen with a small dining table similar to what we have in Bristol and a cosy looking lounge area. We will definitely be looking for a similar place to buy.

I search the cabinets for a glass and fill it with water at the sink before turning out the lights and heading back to the stairs, grabbing my suitcase as I go. Upstairs is just as modern looking as downstairs it has a distinct beachy theme running throughout the cottage and everything you need in a holiday rental. Although there are two bedrooms, I can see immediately which one Raz has chosen. The larger of the two. There is a good-sized double bed that is still in a state of disarray. I drop my suitcase by the door, and the thud it makes as it hits the floor sounds loud in the silent cottage. Flicking on the bedside light, I turn off the main light I used upon entering the room.

I should shower, but I'm so tired, and the emotion of today is catching up with me. There's a lump in my throat as I try to fight down the feelings that want to take over, the panic of hearing Raz was hurt and his painful words when he thought he might not make it. I try to remind myself that he is fine and that we're getting married. Maybe I'll just lie down here for a minute, then get undressed.

–

The wind howling and rattling around the cottage wakes me from a fitful sleep. It's always difficult to get a good night's sleep in a new bed, but I was overtired, emotional, and missing Raz fiercely last night. The bed still smells like him, and I realise as I drag myself awake that I am holding on to his pillow as if it were his body. My arms wrapped around it, cuddling its softness against my chest.

It looks like the weather has turned nasty, judging by the rain that is lashing against the window. I forgot to close the curtains last night or, in fact, do anything. Once I laid down on the bed, I was out like a light, and even though I stirred quite a few times in the night, I didn't have the energy to get off the bed.

I reach over to the bedside table where I left my phone. It's almost out of charge. Swinging my legs over the side of the bed, I stretch before walking over to my bag, which I left by the door. After a quick search and with half the contents of my suitcase on the floor, I find my charger and plug it in, then attach my phone. There's a message from Raz already saying he hasn't slept well as the nurses were checking on him during the night. However, they are saying he should be okay to come back to the rental today. I breathe out a sigh of relief. I hadn't realised just how much hope I was pinning on the doctor's assumption that Raz would be ready to leave today. I send a quick message telling him I've just got up and that I'll speak to him shortly.

First, though, I need to shower, change, eat, and email my boss again. I'm sure he won't be all that happy about me taking the next few weeks off, but I'll offer to work from here on anything that is important. Hopefully, after Tuesday, I can hand in my notice anyway. After shooting another message off to Raz, I pad downstairs in slippered feet, once again grateful that Jay put the heating on a timing schedule; it would be freezing in this old stone building otherwise. I fill the kettle halfway, put it on to boil and search around for the tea and coffee, finding the lovely blue and cream striped Cornishware jars in one of the cupboards.

My phone rings as I'm sitting at the table with a bowl of cereal and a mug of tea, scrolling through social media and waiting for Raz to reply to my last message.

"Ben, I've found it!" Chloe's voice is tinged with excitement as my brain races to catch up with what she is trying to say.

"Found what, Chlo?" I ask, still not quite sure where this is going.

"The perfect place for you and Raz, of course. You can thank me later but get dressed. We are going to see it in an hour on our way to break Raz out of the hospital."

I can hear Marcus' deep laugh down the phone, and I can just imagine Chloe bouncing on one foot and then the other with barely contained excitement.

"Okay, okay, give me thirty minutes to finish my breakfast and then I'll meet you in the pub car park." Now I'm laughing as she whoops with joy and ends the call. I'm still smiling as I hurriedly finish my breakfast and tea, reply to Raz, who has insisted I get him out before lunch is served because the food isn't great there. In keeping with our promise to communicate better, I let Raz know that I'm going to see a house with Chlo today on the way to get him. He's a bit disappointed that he can't come, but we agree that if it's any good, we'll look at it again once I've assessed the accessibility for him as he's in plaster at the moment.

I'm just heading to the door chuckling at the message Chloe sent saying she'd come and get me, when she knocks at the door. I unlock it ushering her in, out of the rain, while I grab my wallet and coat. "Marc's at the pub. He's filling in for a bit today," Chlo says as she waits by the door shaking the droplets of water from her hair. Her raincoat is one of those hikers' ones with the fleece inside and looks to be soaking wet.

"It's filthy weather out there. Has Raz got a decent coat that he can get into?"

Good question. I take a look at the coat on the hook, his lightweight jacket was the one he was wearing yesterday, and that one is toast now.

"This one will have to do. Not sure his plaster will fit through the armhole, though." I look it over sceptically.

"I've got a cast cover somewhere, I think? I used it when my wrist was broken. It might cover some of it at least," Chloe suggests, and I readily agree to drop by her house before we go off to view this cottage she's excited about. Once we have that and are on our way to the cottage, I can't help but ask her how she managed to get us a viewing so quickly.

"Okay, don't freak out, but the old man who lived there died recently, and I bumped into the daughter-in-law in the shops this morning. I mean, I literally ran right into her." Chloe laughs as she steers us onto the main road. "We got to chatting, and I have to admit to being a bit cheeky and asking if we could take a look this morning. She texted her husband, and he seemed okay with it. They are clearing the place out. It's been empty for months."

I might have looked a little freaked out by the fact the guy who owned the house died, but Chlo hastened to add that he didn't actually die in the cottage; he had been in hospital for a while. So I guess that's a little better then. All thoughts along that line go out of my head when we drive down a little dirt track just past a farm and come to the cutest cottage I've ever seen. I can already see a bit of work that's needed a few broken tiles on the roof edges. The garden is overgrown, but the beautiful white stone walls look welcoming even in the pouring rain. Chloe parks the car and turns to me.

"What do you think? First impressions?" She bites her lip, looking like she is trying to stop herself from saying anything as she waits for my opinion.

"I don't want to get my hopes up, Chlo, but it's perfect," I whisper, afraid that if I take my eyes off the place, it will disappear. The light green wooden front door opens, and lovely looking red-haired lady waves at Chloe.

"Come on, let's go and look inside," Chloe says as she gets out of the car before I've even answered. I'm not sure which of us is more excited, and I quickly snap a photo of the outside whilst Chlo keeps the lady busy and send it to Raz. Then I hurry inside after them, where I'm introduced to Lynn and her husband, Robert. I offer my condolences which Robert accepts and states his father had a wonderful life and that this cottage has amazing memories for him and his family. They live further down the coast now in their own piece of paradise, as he put it, and although it's a shame to sell the place, he hasn't got the time to deal with it.

"I'd rather it went to someone who could appreciate the

beauty of the old place," Robert said, looking a little emotional before excusing himself to continue packing up his father's things.

Lynn took us on a grand tour of the place, and I loved every nook and cranny, but I think the place that stole my heart was the lounge. With its stone fireplace and inbuilt log burner, which Lynn said they had installed to make the place easier to heat, but her father-in-law had always complained about the loss of his open fire. This room really has the cosy feel of home about it and makes me want to stay here forever.

"It was just so messy, and he couldn't keep it up. Rob and I were worried that it might spit out and set the place alight as he kept forgetting to put the fireguard in place," Lynn adds as she shows Chloe through to the kitchen.

As you enter the room, on the right-hand side is a seat carved into the very stone of the house underneath a window that looks out across the farmland. I take a picture of that and the log burner. Unfortunately, I can't send them to Raz as I've got no signal inside the house, but I try and commit to memory every wonderful detail. I can imagine our furniture here, a comfy cushion on the window seat for Raz to read his books. This is just perfect.

Of course, the next question is can we afford it? I'm already in love with the place, and I can't help but share this fact with Lynn as I join them in the kitchen. In here, I feel like I've stepped back into the nineteen seventies because the look of the cabinets and stand-alone cooker give off that impression.

"Don't worry about the kitchen; you can refurb," Chlo whispers as soon as Lynn is out of earshot and walking off towards the other end of the kitchen, suggesting we look upstairs. There is a set of stairs set into the stone wall just off of the kitchen, and they look very dark, but with a flick of an old-fashioned switch, the white walls are illuminated by candle-looking lights set into the tiny alcoves up the wall as we climb the stairs. I hear Chlo gasp, and I'm sure my jaw is on the floor. It is stunning.

"I think you will both love the main bedroom," Lynn says as she climbs the stairs ahead of us.

I don't need convincing. This is the perfect place for Raz and me to reconnect and begin to heal.

Our forever home.

Chapter NINETEEN

RAZ

I'm trying not to get impatient waiting for more pictures or texts from Ben. Even from the one message and picture I got when they arrived, I could tell that he loved it, and the cottage looked private and so perfect that it made me feel warm and fuzzy inside. However, that could still be the painkillers because I'm taking those regularly and the world—outside of my impatience to be out of here and with Ben—is rather rosy. I can see a future for us now—I always could, but this one is perfect. Coastal walks, dinners with our best friends, being part of this community and taking life a little slower. Plus the food, oh my goodness, there is some delicious seafood down here, well, not in this hospital, but that's to be expected when they have so many mouths to feed.

Thinking about all the wonderful food is making my mouth water... it's not helped by the smell of food that is wafting into the room. Five out of the six beds in this room are currently occupied, but I haven't made much of an effort to get to know the other occupants as they all look to be a lot more poorly than me. One of the men spent most of the night snoring, that, the discomfort of my plaster, and the regular check-ups by the staff meant little sleep for me, and despite the buzz of the pain meds, I am feeling a bit disgruntled waiting to be picked up so I can get the hell out of here and see my boyfriend finally.

"Well, that's a grumpy looking face, babe." Ben's voice has me looking up from my phone vigil, and as he approaches the bed, I can't contain my excitement at seeing him again. I was going to mess around with him and complain about the amount of time he took to get here but looking at him now, his eyes dancing with joy. I can't.

"Have they signed you off?" he asks, looking around, no doubt to see if there are any staff around. "I told the nurse as I came in that I was here to take you home." Ben leans over, gives me a quick kiss on the forehead and pulls back. I know he's doing that for me. My aversion to public displays of affection has governed how we are with each other when we aren't at home for as long as we've been together, and I can't promise to get on board with a full display of affection, but I'm going to try more.

"I'm good to go as soon as I've got some clothes on." I look hopefully at Ben.

"Lucky I got the bag out of the car then, isn't it." Chloe's voice is unmistakable, and I see Ben's cheeks tinge a little at his forgetfulness.

"Sorry, I was just so eager to get in here and tell Raz about the cottage," Ben says, taking the small bag of my belongings from Chloe, who makes herself comfortable in the chair next to the bed.

"I'll tell you all about it as I help you get into these. Do you want me to take you to the loo? Or just get changed here?" Ben is all business, and I glance over at Chlo, who is raising an eyebrow at the suggestion that I get undressed here, challenging me with her facial expression as she smirks at me.

"Pull the curtain, Chlo. I'll get dressed here." I wink at her accepting the challenge. It's not like she hasn't seen me in my boxers before but naked. Nope, not something we've… My thought trails off as I remember the time I did see her naked and battered.

"Don't even go there." Ben's words are whispered in my ear for only me to hear. He reads me like a book, this man of mine.

Nodding, I stand with Ben's assistance, and between us, we manage to get me dressed into some joggers, a T-shirt and partially into my coat. Unfortunately, the sleeves of my hoodies aren't big enough, so my damaged arm is underneath my hoodie, with the coat on top of it to protect me from the weather as much as possible.

"We'll find some clothes that fit tomorrow, babe," Ben

reassures me.

"I wore oversized hoodies. It might work for you?" Chloe suggests as the nurse arrives with my prescriptions, a few dos and don'ts about my injuries and a wheelchair to get me to the car.

The trip back to the cottage was uneventful and a little uncomfortable. I had to move the front seat back pretty far to accommodate my plaster. Ben was full of excitement about the place he had been to see with Chlo, and I couldn't help but smile at his enthusiasm. Chlo dropped us as close to the rental cottage as she could get. It was still a considerable effort to manoeuvre the wheelchair we borrowed from the hospital through the cottage door. Finally, I was able to put my leg up and lie down on the sofa. Ben lit the log burner, and I began to relax as he put the kettle on and fixed me a sandwich.

"Okay, babe, I'm thinking we can try and get you upstairs after this, so you are closer to the loo, but we might need to re-think staying in the cottage for the next few weeks until your plaster is off?" Ben hands me the sandwich and settles in one of the sofa chairs near the log burner with his own.

"Chlo said she'd chat with Jay to see if he has or knows of any more accessible places for us to stay for now," he adds, looking thoughtful. Neither of us has ever had to deal with this issue before, so this is all new, and there appears to be many obstacles in front of us. One of which is work.

"I can work from home, but what about you? You can't take that much time off work, Ben."

I'm not sure that I want him to return to Bristol without me, but what else can we do? I start to chew the ham sandwich he made, trying to come up with solutions. I might manage better in Bristol because we have an ensuite bathroom but getting up and down the stairs to make food will be a problem when Ben is at work.

"I can almost hear your mind working from over here, babe. Stop worrying. We'll think of something, and as for work, I've told them I'll be out for a few weeks, and I'll work from home." Ben gets up and takes my plate into the kitchen, then hands me the tea he put down on the side table when he returns.

"You are my priority, Raz. Now let me show you the photos I took of that cottage. I think you are going to love it."

The rest of the day is spent talking about the future, and as Ben predicted, I fell in love with the cottage straight away. We put an offer on it and contacted an estate agent in Bristol to discuss putting our house on the market. Chlo popped in with Marc in the evening, bringing with them a takeaway. It was perfect, and knowing how close the new cottage that we both love is to where they live, has made this sort of evening a possibility for the future. I can't help but feel content, even if I am a bit uncomfortable at the moment. Ben managed to help me up the stairs and down again with the help of Marc when I needed the loo earlier, but now we are on our own

A BRIDGE TO FOREVER

I'm worried that we won't make it upstairs again.

"We'll take it one step at a time, babe, and head straight for the bathroom." Ben is all business as we make our way to the staircase. "Chlo said Jay may know of a place we can rent instead of this one for the next few weeks. It's a bungalow, so everything is on one level." He continues to chat as I focus on holding on to the bannister and him as we make our way unsteadily up to the second floor.

"I'll take it from here," I state firmly as he helps me to the bathroom. There are some things I need to learn to do for myself. I'm already annoyed with being so reliant on Ben.

"Okay, but let me help you undress, then I'm going to get you washed. I've ordered a plaster cover to arrive at Chlo's house tomorrow. That one she lent us is great for your arm, but we need one for your leg so you can shower." Ben says as he helps me get my T-shirt and joggers off. "Want these off too?" He asks, sliding his fingers under the waistband of my boxer briefs, and I look down at where his fingers are touching me, feeling my cock start to stir. Highly inappropriate at this point in time. Not even sure that I have it in me for anything other than a cuddle tonight, but my dick is begging to differ.

"Yes." *Was that my voice?* The word sounds so breathy. Did it suddenly get hot in here? Ben slides my boxers off my legs, over the plaster and onto the floor. I look down at him on the floor at my feet, and I swear all my blood runs into my cock. He looks up at me with a smirk; he knows what he's doing to me. I manage to shoo him out of the bathroom momentarily. I'm just starting to wash using a cloth he left on the sink when he comes back. Totally naked.

"You were supposed to wait for me." He pretends to be cross, but I can see the glint of amusement in his eyes as he shuts the bathroom door and walks toward me. I watch in the mirror as he comes to stand behind me at the sink. The heat from his body sends tiny electric shocks through me before he's even touched me. Our eyes connect in the mirror as he takes the washcloth from me and gently cleans my face using the mirror to guide his movements. The bruising on my body has started to show more, all purple and angry. Ben winces as he guides the cloth over them.

"I thought I was going to lose you." His admission breaks the silent tension between us as he rinses the cloth in the warm water I had run in the sink, and he begins to stroke my neck with the cloth. My eyelids close as I let my head fall back, allowing him better access as he moves closer, his body caging me in against the sink. "I never want to feel that way again." His voice is husky as he breathes his words onto my neck, and I feel his lips touch the skin below my ear, sending a shiver of anticipation through my aching body. Sure everything hurts right now, but more important than that is the throbbing between my legs as need for this man overtakes everything else.

The washcloth continues its journey around my body as he washes every inch of me, kissing my skin intermittently and raising my awareness of his obvious arousal when he holds me against him. The cloth is abandoned as Ben uses a fluffy white towel to dry me. This intimate attention is causing my senses to go into overdrive, and I realise I haven't said a word since he started. My breath leaves my lips in a loud exhale as Ben's body comes into contact with mine again, and I look into the mirror to see him watching me. His blue eyes are hooded by lids that speak of his need, and his hard cock presses against me, just shy of where I need it.

"Ben, I'm so sorry I put you through that." I look into the mirror at him, face next to mine, looking over my shoulder at me in the glass. His arm snakes around under mine and across my chest. Splaying his hand out on my collarbone, he pulls me hard against him. His teeth nip my shoulder, and my hips jerk forward at the sensation. Ben looks at me through his lashes. The air around us is full of charge, or at least it feels like it is to me. The anticipation is killing me. Will he let go? Or is he too afraid of hurting me to take this further? Right now, I'm not even aware of my injuries, only the man whose hard length is pressed against my arse cheeks. If I move a little this way...

"Raz," he growls. His words are pained and needy. "Fuck, babe, I don't want to hurt you." He grips my shoulder tight, and his other hand, which has found its way to my hip, pulls me against him harder, at odds with his words that suggest he doesn't want to take this any further. I understand what he is saying, but perhaps he just needs a little something to tip him over the edge so that he can satisfy this desperate aching need I have for him. Bending my hips slightly, I lean a little over the sink, gripping it with my good hand and resting the plaster on the surface with the other. I look at him in the mirror as his eyes start to darken with lust. "You need to stop that, babe, or I'm going to give you what your body is asking for, and I'm not sure you are ready for that." His Adam's apple bobs as he swallows, his struggle evident as, even as he says the words, trying hard to do the right thing, his cock slides between my arse cheeks, causing a moan to release from my lips. I say nothing, just watch him in the mirror. I can see the need that shines in his eyes is mirrored in my own. My pupils are blown, and my breathing is heavy as I wait to see if Ben will lose the fight with himself.

My eyes squeeze shut again as Ben's hand moves from my hip around my body and finds my dick, thick and in desperate need of his touch. His grip is punishing as he rubs his thumb over the head and smears pre-cum across it. I grunt out unintelligible sounds as Ben slowly moves his tight hold up and down. Not hard enough to hurt, but the sensations coursing through my body have now amped up, and I'm on fire.

Fuck it, I'll beg, anything to get what I need. "Baby, please."

A resounding slap echo's through the tiny tiled bathroom, and a cry escapes from my lips, part surprise, part pain, part primal, as Ben smacks my arse and shakes his head a little moving away from me. I go to straighten up, a little annoyed that he's not going to take it further.

"Don't fucking move. I would have preferred to take it slow and gentle, maybe just hold you in my arms, but someone around here just can't behave." He bloody winks at me, but I can see from his expression that he is deadly serious, and a strangled sound escapes from me as I anticipate what's to come. Hopefully, me, because I'm seconds away from exploding with all the sexual tension bouncing off the walls. I don't move, though. I just follow Ben with my eyes as he disappears out of the door, only to return seconds later with a bottle of lube. Oh, hell yes.

"You sure this is what you want?" he asks, gliding his gaze over my body, no doubt registering every injury, every tiny cut or bruise. I know full well that if I had changed my mind, he would have backed off, no questions asked.

"Yes." I manage to breathe out the word, not caring about my injuries and more intent on getting what I want.

We don't need any further words. His look as he crosses the room in two strides says it all. He won't be asking again. He flips the bottle's cap off and discards it on the floor, placing the lube on the sink. I lose sight of his movements for a second, and then Ben's fingers under my chin jerk my head around for an all-consuming kiss. His tongue demands that I open to him, and I oblige, willingly submitting to his unspoken request. I feel his other hand slide down my side, leaving goosebumps on my skin; as he reaches my arse, he grabs a handful and massages it in time with the movement of his tongue. My body aches and, despite the pain medication, there is some pain from my ribs, but I choose to ignore it, preferring to chase the high that this man behind me is capable of giving.

Ben breaks our kiss and reaches for the bottle. I exhale as the cold gel touches my needy hole. Ben wastes no time sliding his fingers inside me. His other hand holds tight to my hip as he begins to fuck me with his fingers, moaning his need against my back as my skin is peppered in kisses; his stubble adds to the sensation as he licks and gently bites. I jolt forward with every new touch, my cock bobbing and straining in need of relief. As short, rapid breaths race from my lips, I look in the mirror and lock eyes with Ben as he straightens and watches me over my shoulder. I'm not sure what he is looking for, but whatever it is, I think he finds it as he withdraws his fingers and instantly replaces them with the thick head of his cock. I breathe through it, trying to relax as Ben inches his way inside me, filling me, stretching me.

"You feel so damn good, babe. That's it, relax. Oh yeah, just like that." His words of encouragement have me pushing back into him, wanting all of his hard length inside me. Ben takes it slow, sliding in deep and then pulling back so I can only feel the blunt head of his cock inside me. Fuck, it's like exquisite torture, and I'm down for that. "Look at me," he demands. I didn't realise I'd hung my head as I panted out curses with each slow thrust. I look up into the mirror. His stare is so intense, and I can see from the tightness of his jaw just how much it is taking for him to go this slow. To be this careful with me. My heart swells with love for the man intent on bringing me pleasure without hurting my already battered body.

Chapter TWENTY

BEN

Fucking bliss, that's the only way I can describe the feeling of being inside my man. All thoughts of how I nearly lost him are being purged from my mind with each thrust of my hips. Even though the tension in my muscles is killing me, I refuse to go any faster, wanting to savour every moment and desperate to make sure I don't hurt him. I know he thinks he can take it, but his body is already battered and bruised, and I haven't missed the little twinges of pain that cross his face when the movement pulls on his ribs or other injuries.

My fingers flex on his hips as I attempt to keep my grip reasonably light. Raz curses me between pants as I bring him to the edge and pull back again. Pinpricks of sweat emerge over his back as he takes each thrust with a moan attempting to push back into me and cause me to snap. I know his game, and usually, I would play it happily but not today.

"Cut that out or I'll stop," I grit out between my teeth as I almost lose my fight to be gentle.

"Ben. Fuck!" he cries out as I push into him in one slow thrust. Balls deep, I hold still, pull him up against me so I can reach around and get my hand on him. He's rock hard and swollen, leaking all over my thumb as I rub back and forth. I pump his cock with a lethal grip as I slowly move inside him. The connection between us seems surreal, otherworldly. I can barely breathe with the intensity of the feelings coursing through my body.

"Come for me, babe. I want to hear you scream my name." No sooner do the words whispered near his ear leave my mouth than Raz tenses and cries out my name, groaning and swearing as hot cum coats my hand, still fisting his cock. The sound is my undoing, and with one last thrust, I find my own release as I collapse against him momentarily, barely remembering my own name, let alone that he is injured and can't take my weight.

Quickly I pull back, sliding out of him slowly as he clenches around me, groaning and shaking.

"Fuck, Raz? Did I hurt you?" Stupid idiot, I should have taken him to bed. More to the point, I shouldn't have tried anything in the first place.

"The next words out of your mouth had better not be an apology, baby, or we will be having words. That was fucking amazing. I just need to lie down now, though," he admits, and I reach for the cloth abandoned in the sink. Run warm water through it and hurriedly clean him off as best I can before grabbing the clean boxer briefs I brought in earlier. It seems like hours that we've been in the bathroom.

"I'll get you settled on the bed before I shower." I help him back to the bedroom and get him onto the bed, where he assures me he will stay. Then rush back to the bathroom to clean up and shower as fast as I can. Needing to be back in the bedroom with Raz and holding him.

As I dry off, I can hear him on the phone with someone, and when I wander into the bedroom, he has the cutest smile on his face, which just gets bigger as he sees me. He's also on my phone rather than his, which makes me curious.

"Yes, that's great. Thank you for calling. No, it's okay; we weren't asleep. That's great news, thanks." As he ends the call, I continue to wait, standing there in just a towel.

"That was Lynn. She and Robert have had a discussion and want to accept our offer. Obviously, we need surveys and to find the best way to deal with this sale as it wasn't with an estate agent, but Robert knows a solicitor who might be able to help, and they should be able to recommend one for us." His eyes dance with joy as he puts the phone down and holds his hand out to me. I take it willingly, loving the look of excitement on his face. He hasn't even physically seen the place, but he already wants it. Because he trusts me and my judgment, that's a heady thing to have, his trust.

"This is it, baby. The start of our new life together."

I kneel on the bed next to him, careful not to jostle him

any more than he has already been. Kissing him gently on the lips, I try to show some restraint even if it's a little too late for that. Only Raz isn't having any of that; his hand pulls at the nape of my neck, holding me to him as his tongue licks across my lips. A groan escapes me, which he uses as his in to plunder my mouth, and I go willingly, lying on the bed next to him, trying to keep control of the situation and failing miserably. My need for this man is never-ending, and we are both breathless by the end of our kiss.

"I can't wait for this, Raz. It's what I need. What we need to move forward. I'm sure of it." I rest my forehead against his before collapsing next to him on the bed. We lie side by side, looking at each other, and I reach out, stroking his face gently, aware of every cut and bruise that he has. I've memorised every single one, knowing that I am so lucky to have him by my side still.

"Will you be okay with leaving your family, Ben? It's a big step with all that's going on right now."

He's mentioned this already, and I think I need to reiterate that this is because of them, because of what happened. I need to move forward with the man I love and not waste another second in a job that I don't love in an area that doesn't hold the same appeal to me as it once did.

"The cottage has two spare rooms. One will make a fantastic guest room and the other we can use as a study. We might even be able to put a blow-up bed in there, but I'm not sure if it would fit yet. If we had a few guests. There are always the rooms at the pub too." I want to show him that I've thought this through, and I honestly believe this is the right move for us.

"It's just like a dream come true, and if I weren't in plaster and aching all over, I would think that I had fallen asleep and that none of this is real." He looks so earnest as if he is half expecting to wake up, and we are back in Bristol, still in the darkness. Pulling myself up onto my elbow, I lean in closer and take his lips with mine.

"Does that feel real?" My words are low, intimate. I stroke my fingers down his jaw and onto his chest, watching as goosebumps appear on his skin. Then I remind myself that we are both almost naked in an old cottage in late autumn, and the heating has gone off. Chuckling at my thoughts, I pull back and run a thumb along the lip that has now pouted on his face bringing a smile out instead. Then busy myself getting us ready for bed and turning off the ceiling light, leaving only the lamp on my bedside table.

Once we are both tucked under the duvet, I turn to him again. Leaning over him slightly so I can see his eyes better.

"Marry me?" I ask.

"Have you forgotten that you've already asked, and I said yes?" Raz smiles at me, chuckling slightly.

"No, I just wanted to hear you say it again." My lips curl up in an answering smile.

"Yes, a thousand times yes. I will marry you, baby." His eyes twinkle with joy, and that's what I needed to see. I guess

I hadn't realised that I was worried that his acceptance of my proposal was to do with his near-death experience. Here, now, in the safety of our bed. Just us together. I can see that he means it. He wants to be mine forever, just as I will be his.

Epilogue

BEN

"Hurry up, slowcoach. Raz will get there before us at this rate." Elle's voice is full of laughter as she tries to get me to hurry. I straighten my tie again for what seems like the thousandth time feeling nervous as hell.

"I'm ready. Okay, let's do this." I take one final look in the mirror, admiring my grey suit and lilac tie, with a matching pocket square.

"You look fantastic. Now, let's move." Elle grabs my arm, pulling me out of the hotel room where I stayed last night. Chlo had insisted that we spend the night before our wedding apart, so she made Raz stay with her and Marc. We indulged her, thankful for all the help not only Chloe and Marc have given us but also Lou, Jay, Tilly, and Con. Over the last months, they have become like family to us, helping us whilst Raz was incapacitated and finding us a place to stay that was easier for him to get around. Ferrying him about when I had to go back to Bristol to pack up and sort out selling our house. It has been a total whirlwind, and in all that, we have managed to plan a small wedding.

Neither of us wanted to wait, so we booked this hotel which is a few miles away from Pendlebrook but has a stunning view of the ocean in the room they use for weddings. My family have also been amazing, helping as much as they can from Bristol. Even Jen, who I thought wouldn't want to come, got stuck in saying she needed the distraction. I'm not sure what happened between her and Matt, but he is now living back at Pendlebrook with his dad. He left shortly after he helped move her into a new flat.

I haven't been there yet with all that is going on, but Mum and Dad weren't all that keen on the area she's moved to. They even offered for her to live with them for the time being whilst her house is waiting to be sold, but of course, she refused.

Elle squeezes my cheeks between her hands, pulling my focus back to her smiling face.

"Second thoughts?" She laughs at her joke, and I can't help but roll my eyes at her, but I answer anyway.

"Never!" I reply, trying to sound insulted, but I just end up laughing along with her as we enter the room with floor-to-ceiling windows that give a fantastic view of the bay below. It may be winter still, but the sun has decided to shine, and it lends a glow to this warm room. White and lilac fabric cover the chairs, which stand in rows, and as I walk down between them, I nod and smile at our family and friends. Charlie and Aiden are also here, looking stunning in their suits; their faces show genuine happiness for us. They have turned out to be excellent friends, and with their help, Raz and I have found a counsellor close by our new house. We are seeing her separately and together as a couple which has made such a difference and is helping us heal.

We invited them down for Christmas to the place we rented whilst our house sale went through, and I am sure they will be regular visitors now.

"You ready?" My dad stands beside me, looking smart in his grey suit, and I glance over at Mum in the front row. She is beaming at us both, dabbing a tissue to the corner of her eye and clutching Jen's hand. Jen is looking much better. Her eyes still carry her sorrow, but outwardly she has improved greatly. However, I know Elle, Mum, and Dad are keeping a careful eye on her. She isn't coming back to Pendlebrook after the wedding because the memories are still too much for her. She has been so brave, and I'm just grateful to have her here today. We are all staying at this hotel tonight, and Mum and Dad will drive back with her tomorrow. Elle is staying down here with Jim and the kids for a few days. I look over at them now, and the smile on my face pulls at my cheeks. Elle is trying to get the kids to sit still, but they are fidgeting with their formal wear, far too used to wearing casual clothes.

"Yes, I'm ready," I answer Dad, remembering his

question and pulling my gaze away from my family. My heart swells with love at the intimate wedding we have managed to arrange in such a short space of time. It feels perfect. Even Stu has made it with a few of my closer colleagues from my old job. My boss isn't among them. I'm not sure he's forgiven me for leaving yet, but I am so damn happy with the new job I really don't care.

The first bars of a classical rendition of John Legend's "All of Me" has me standing up straight and homing my attention to the back of the room, as everyone goes silent. Anticipation fills me, and I try to keep my feet still as the large wooden door at the back opens, and then he's there. Walking in with Chloe, arms linked, his lilac suit a match for the colour of my tie. Raz's tie is grey and tied in a Winchester knot setting off his waistcoat and jacket. He looks spectacular, not just because of what he is wearing, but because his tanned skin is glowing with health. I get lost in his deep brown eyes as he approaches, barely limping, almost fully recovered apart from the odd scar.

Raz stops just as he reaches me, and Chloe, who is dressed in a lilac suit jacket with a matching skirt and light grey blouse, reaches up and gives him a quick hug, then winks at me before joining Marc in the front row at the other side of the room.

Raz's hand is warm in mine as he grips it briefly, and then we stand side by side, looking out over the ocean as the registrar begins the wedding ceremony. Joining us legally in a way that our hearts have been joined from the very beginning. I repeat the words meaning every single one, and get lost in his gaze once more as he repeats the same. We promise to love each other forever, but we are already bound, not by words or law but by our souls.

Dear READER...

Hi, there, beautiful readers. I hope you loved Raz and Ben's story as much as I did. These two decided one day whilst I was in the shower to tell me their story. I lost them for a little while, but then they came back loud and clear.

If you have read the Beyond the Tide trilogy, you will already know them and the other characters from this book. It was wonderful to work in that world again with all the familiar faces, and I hope that you enjoy being back there too, or maybe you are now curious to meet them all properly?

This book is the link between my Beyond the Tide trilogy and the two books that I have coming out next. I had already started to write stories for Matt and Jen, who are featured in this book. These were two separate stories, and I had no idea Jen was related to Ben until he told me. It was a complete surprise, as most of my stories are. I am a total pantser, so whilst I may start with a vague idea of where a book will go, the characters inevitably decide to take a completely different direction.

As with my other books, I have had to speed up the healing process to keep the story moving. Hopefully, I have done them justice. Please remember that these characters, their experiences and the places they visit are, for the most part, completely fiction, and I cannot be held responsible for the way they behave. I simply write it as they tell me!

If you want to keep up to date with what I'm writing, please join my Facebook Group, N Dune's Readers Pod and/or follow me on Instagram. I am also on Amazon, Tik Tok, Bookbub and Goodreads.

I am a self-published Indie author, and like all self-published authors, we love receiving reviews. It also helps our books to be put in front of other readers who may enjoy them, especially if you review them on Amazon. So if you did love this book or any of the others that I have written, please consider leaving a review.

Lastly, I need to thank my Beta readers, Street Team and ARC readers, as well as my amazing editor and my other author friends for being with me on this journey and holding my hand when things get a little tough. I love you all.

Much Love,
N Dune

OTHER BOOKS BY N DUNE

<u>BEYOND THE TIDE TRILOGY:</u>

ESCAPE BEYOND THE TIDE

FOUND BEYOND THE TIDE

CHASED BEYOND THE TIDE

<u>PARANORMAL/FANTASY ROMANCE:</u>

WITHIN HER MAGIC

Printed in Great Britain
by Amazon